CONTENTS

Preface

In his youth Japes was affectionately referred to as J P. For some unknown reason he was the only one in a brood of five blessed with a nickname. It had no real consequences and sometimes appeared easier to simply yell out these two consonants rather than use his full name. Most likely this explained the reason as his parents constantly attempted to keep him "out of trouble".

Visiting the family every summer at Conifer became an annual ritual for his cousins. This is where their mother spent her youth, living in a beautiful two hundred acre resort located at the foothills of the White Mountains.

One summer when he was nine years old the ten children, five boys and five girls, were out playing whiffle ball when his uncle summoned the boys for their haircuts. Everyone received a military haircut referred to at the time as a butch. All of the boys enjoyed this style, including JP's brother. Uncle Roy, a rugged, handsome man, with a disposition the antithesis of JP's father, insisted JP trim his long wavy curls into shape exactly like everyone else. So intimidated by this authoritative urging JP immediately came to tears, as he most definitely did not wish to have this discerning style eliminated from his persona.

Aside from his father there was only one other person who could bring peace to this unrivaled calamity. Aunt

Keinath had an elegant way of making one feel welcome and comfortable, she called him Japes instead of JP, and with a gentle smile said, "Your hair looks fine just the way it is". She then introduced this lad to a fantastic food that he had never tried before. In fact, the sausage, not sold in that area of the country, would forever become one of his favorites. She filled his belly with linguicia and an ice-cold glass of lemonade. Within a half hour this wonderful woman had turned an awkward nickname into something cool, had approved of his signature hairdo, and filled him up with a food he loves to this day.

Aunt Keinath was the only person to ever refer to this youngster as Japes. It made him feel special and brought a smile to his face as well as comfort to his soul. On his journey through life he felt the same warmth every time he set foot into a new hotel. This was his adventure.

The Marion Hotel

Japes could not stop smiling as he entered the hotel world. The scene was magnificent as everyone scurried about taking care of business. Racers constantly darted back and forth. They were distinct in appearance with slender, wiry frames and fast purposeful movements. For some reason the Racers always dominated the lobby scene, Japes did not know why, but he became fascinated with the behavior. Some of the Racers were on their way to lunch, while others were tending to their business affairs. The entire lobby bustled with activity, and the Racers were not alone. Although not large in number, the Bulls appeared distinct in their disposition, they were not tall or short, nor did they have any special color or pattern to their bodies. Their vibrant demeanor reminded him of the cocktail hour hosted by his parents at his family resort. The Bulls seemed to be overweight every single one of them. Holding court in various parts of the public space, always surrounded by their minions, appeared to be the norm. No two individuals were exactly the same, and in fact all were unique. The initial observation of this handful of separate but distinct behaviors displayed by patrons and servers alike was more than a simple curiosity. It indeed exhibited a measure by which individuals lived and represented a commonality in their interaction with others. In the nomad existence, inevitable for

4

the dedicated server to 'hone one's craft,' this emerged as a relentless theme to the world within the hotel. The actual fulfillment of security, empowerment, and simple relaxation to patrons often times juxtaposed those who served, and this reality was questioned at every step of his journey.

What a thrill for him to see all the different patrons, as he had been learning his entire life and could not wait to start. The anticipation to see and learn was almost too much to fathom. Ms. Pinky, the orientation lady, old and crotchety with a distinctive limp and a wry grin spoke just like a grammar school teacher. "Now come along everyone do not stare at our guests and stay in a group". He did not know what kind of server Ms. Pinky represented, but she sure had a weird name. As they took the corner into a room adjacent to the main lobby everyone stopped dead in their tracks. A cinema star entered the front door accompanied by his entourage. Seeing celebrities on television or in the movies was one thing, but now, here, not five feet from them, larger-than-life, emerged Bill Cosby one of the best comedians in the world. He regularly stayed at the hotel, and it became apparent he made plenty of friends. In fact, a number of cinema stars frequented the establishment by virtue of the hotel's close proximity to a well-known nightclub.

Ms. Pinky quickly motioned for everyone to continue the orientation tour passing the main entrance towards the front office. The main entrance stood grand displaying a large red carpet with an immaculately attired elderly man greeting everyone. On the west side of the lobby, a bar with an enormous stone fireplace, highlighted in the background by a spectacular view of the High Country Mountains, acted as a magnet drawing in the wayward traveler. " Are guests allowed to sit here and enjoy a cocktail?" asked Japes. "But of course", replied Ms. Pinky "That is the whole idea". Just trying to be nice Ms. Pinky, he thought to himself, realizing it was not necessary to speak. The bar itself looked beautiful, welcoming patrons with elegant hand carved stools displaying seashell inlays made of driftwood for seating. The actual bar was constructed of an emerald green stone polished as smooth as a baby's bottom. A girl named Mary tended the bar. "Hi to everyone and enjoy the day", she winked at Japes as he passed by.

Some of the guests were drinking, but most were just taking in the view. The rest of the lobby appeared immaculate with various seating arrangements; telephones were available throughout as many guests made business calls. This was primarily a hotel for the business traveler. As the group proceeded toward the front desk, Ms. Pinky waived at a guest service agent, he pushed a button, allowing everyone access through a side door next to the desk. Ms. Pinky said, "This is where it all happens in a hotel, the brains of the operation. Everyone who stays here must interact with this office as all inquiries, guest charges and registration go through here!" The office, nothing fancy, appeared to be the opposite of the public space, with long and narrow glossy black walls. One fairly large room housed eight servers taking reservations for future arrivals. They were all Round Bottom servers with wide hips; he had never seen so many in one area. They sat all day long and typed giving them the distinct attribute of large round bottoms. The telephone operator's area, immediately adjacent, staffed four servers who constantly toiled with the communication duties. Hundreds of small strips of paper were used to keep track of all the guests. Each guest had their name and room number on one of these slips, and they were all alphabetically listed on a large spindle standing in the middle of the room. Daily, the slips would be changed as customers arrived and departed, there were well over one thousand guests in-house that day.

Further down the hall stood a small sterile cash room where, behind a grated opening, a young Flathead server known as the general cashier, counted the days take. The staff's banks were kept in this nook and the cashier provided them change. As they moved further down the hall, located on a large shelving unit, sat a sophisticated video station. It held the in- room "Spankvision" recording files where rows and rows of movie tapes were housed with various cinema stars promoting their movies. Finally, Pinky snuck everyone out onto the stage and wow, what a busy scene it was with five servers in constant motion. Registering new guests and changing the room-board with these little paper strips from vacant to occupied and vice versa remained consistent. They were checking the bucket to see if it agreed with the board. The bucket contained a file where each customer's charges were stored, thus requiring the cashier and the desk manager to actively monitor the arrivals and departures. The amount of work done by these servers was incredible, especially in terms of the dexterity needed to keep track of all these papers. The superior servers could orchestrate these duties while maintaining eye contact with and engaging new guests. Before they left the stage, Japes asked the desk manager "Why do you keep a mechanical counter in your hand?" The perfectly attired man looked at him in a condescending manner "Obviously this is how we keep track of our occupancy for the day". It was his way of saying, you little insignificant gnat, do not bother me. As they started to leave Japes turned to the future server next to him and whispered, "Maybe if he clicked that counter enough his zipper would magically zip up". They went on their way laughing at the pompous ass, as he continued to work with his fly laying halfway open.

THE WORLD

The group continued walking to the back of the hotel. This inside world they entered included the employee entrance, the time clock, and under no circumstances could anyone ever enter or exit from any other doorway. Next, they strolled through the cafeteria and the employee locker room. Impressed by the cafeteria, they perused the daily specials, salad bar, and soda fountain. If one did not like the entrée the kitchen staff graciously prepared a grilled cheese or a hamburger sandwich. Appearing to be larger than it actually was, the room displayed a large bank of windows overseeing the courtyard, while the ancient Flat Top cast the smell of burgers, grilled cheese, and home fried potatoes throughout. The servers took a full half-hour break whenever possible. Red brick walls and white window treatments perfectly matched the checkered tablecloths creating a true refuge for those needing to escape the public eye.

The enormous uniform room housed doorman's suits, bellman's suits, waiter and waitress uniforms, as well as front office blazers. Japes received a forty-two long, navy blue one hundred percent polyester no wrinkle blazer with gold buttons. Landing a real job paying five dollars per hour with an official uniform marked his beginning. Next, stoping by both the resident and general managers' offices truly thrilled the entourage. The resident manager did not actually

9

live there, but he oversaw the entire room operations, including the housekeeping, front office, bell stand, and maintenance departments. A Kiva in training, working to become a true manager, Mr. Cribs dressed perfectly, attired in a blue wool pinstripe suit looking and acting as if he owned the hotel. A know it all with the aristocratic air of a British dignitary. Japes found him to be a little pompous and condescending, but, as he would learn, that demonstrated how most Kiva's, more commonly known as a brown nose server survived. This represented their only real means of becoming an executive.

Now Mr. Rosh, the General Manager, office and demeanor were both quite different. A huge man in all the senses, with enormous features including a long chin reminiscent of Herman Munster, his deep, soft voice resonated within his inner sanctum in an extraordinary grand office located deep in the heart of the hotel. The administrator's desk and entry foyer were immaculate with everything placed in exactly the correct position. Mr. Rosh's desk was immense, created from the finest quality mahogany, moreover, the office itself, perfectly appointed from pictures of international dignitaries shaking his hand to a gold desk lamp impressed everyone. It felt intimidating to the uninitiated and created a formal culture. Always to the point and extremely confident with his decisions, he constantly reminded all that this was his world and he ruled

10

everyone and everything in it, eternally preaching the Marion Hotel philosophy how each and every action relied on a "standard operating procedure" and all guest circumstances had been anticipated. If you worked hard and did as you were told then you would be a success. After all, you worked for the best hotel company in the world, and Japes could not wait to get started.

The hotel, situated in an ideal part of the city, bordered an upscale neighborhood relatively close to the highway. The Mountain High City beheld a majestic view of the great divide. The hotel energy revolved around the behavior in this world as servers would thrive within this domain and whoever entered experienced the energy. Feeling special and being pampered resulted in a constant flow of satisfied patrons. There were many worlds similar to the hotels' but none quite the same, for the unseen empowerment when properly presented was powerful and truly remarkable. The outside world revealed an entirely different story.

The first full day at work started at eleven PM. All new desk staff started on the graveyard shift, as the best way to learn all the inner workings of the business occurred at night. Japes would not be working on just one task he would have to do a little bit of everything. He became a "jack of all trades" and a master problem solver.

11

Early on he learned that the guest was always right and that he must satisfy their needs. Realizing that everyone acted differently in a hotel as compared to being at home, gave credence to the practice of special treatment, and the finest hotels did exactly this. The night shift in this busy city hotel required enormous skill in diplomacy when walking guests. "Walking a guest," meant telling someone with a guaranteed reservation that they did not have a room, a most difficult skill to master especially when one was instructed to satisfy their needs. A bit of a mental predicament for him as it went against everything he had learned.

A natural at this duty came to light when he walked fifteen guests on his first night alone, miraculously not angering any of the guests. One guest in particular came at him hard. A small man with large horn rimmed glasses impatiently waited in line. The type you see at the supermarket questioning the price of a can of peas while the multitudes stood in line. "You mean to tell me you only have one room for me!" he screamed. "I know I have two reservations I even have a confirmation number." "Yes Mr. Spam your reservation is for one room. I'm sorry we do not have any more available rooms," he replied. "You mean if Mr. Marion came through that door, he would not get a room!" If Mr. Marion walked through that door, he would give him a medal for putting up with this obstinate pinhead. Nobody in their right mind would take this abuse if they could accommodate. " That's right Mr. Spam I couldn't even give the owner a room, and frankly Mr. Spam I would inconvenience someone else just to help you, but the truth is you have the last room in the hotel. Is that the truth? Yes, and if you wish, I will find two rooms for you at another hotel and we will pay for them, or you can take the one remaining room for you and your business partner". He leaned over the counter and spoke. "Mr. Spam the seventy five year-old lady behind you has been coming here for years. She visits her family in town. I know she doesn't want me to walk her, would you like to relocate? Finally, after ten minutes of debate, "I will assume you are being honest and I will take the room." stated Mr.Spam. Of course he couldn't have cared less about the lady he just wanted another room. And so it went, Japes walked corporate travelers and even though the hotel would pay for their relocation, they would not care, as the expense belonged to the company and the real importance rested with the location of their meetings and appointments. Despite these obstacles, the gift of empathy and honesty proved to be appropriate in these matters.

This beginning lasted nearly three months, a long period for a new hire. Nothing had opened up during the day shifts, and it became apparent that he had handled the difficult graveyard shifts so well that the brass hesitated to make a change. Now the hierarchy of servers in the front

13

office starts with the front office manager, the assistant manager, the desk manager, and the spanker more commonly known as a supervisor. Like all common servers the hope was to someday evolve into the true leader of a hotel. This is the same in all hotel worlds, and although Japes, sat at the bottom of the chain, he overflowed with ambition and confidence.

The third shift became fascinating, as he grew more familiar with the true flavor of the nights. A number of hookers frequented the desk on a regular basis. Meeting a "lady of the evening" for the first time was an education in itself, as they always asked to cash hundred dollar travelers-checks at all hours of the night. He cashed thousands of dollars during his tenure on the night shift, and thought nothing of it, as none of the Flatheads ever mentioned a problem. Well, after cashing a bunch, for a girl named Judy, he recognized that the travelers-checks were under different names. The naïve hotelier realized that Judy earned a lucrative living going from pad to pad soliciting a little belly bumping from any willing guest. A fruitful gig until the vice show up one night. Japes told Judy "You need to be careful the cops are on to you". "Thanks kid, but don't worry," she replied. He had no reason to anguish he sort of liked her and wanted to protect her from being arrested. Judy was a petite girl with a beautiful smile and a dark, sumptuous complexion;

she wore little makeup and compared to the other painted up ladies of the evening she truly stood alone.

The whole scene was a pile of crap so they, "the vice", cleaned up the nightclub and public space as undercover cops caught Judy and the other hustlers. One week later everyone returned playing the same game, but with a much greater commitment to discretion. The bellmen, doormen, and bartenders hooked up the guests by making a call. This subtle and less conspicuous avenue changed nothing, except there would be no cashing of checks at the desk, no walking the halls, and no drinking in the clubs. Appearing like nothing had ever happened, these amazing tactics revealed that everyone could, in a heartbeat, change their behavior, something that would never occur in the outside world.

One night a server in training named Ozer came running to the desk all in a panic. Ozer, maybe eighteen years old from a small town in the Plains-land, defined rural. He looked like the scarecrow from the Wizard of Oz with a little less straw, but plenty of freckles. He had not known it yet, but he liked boys more than girls. During his shift, his duties included checking a couple of guest rooms that were discrepant. The front office, not sure if the rooms were occupied or vacant, directed him to investigate. Well, one of the suites was definitely occupied, as a naked hooker lay posing on the bed. Ozers' first real view of a beautiful woman arranged for a VIP guest allowed Japes to provide

Ozer with his own orientation. "You just met your first five hundred dollar hooker that Playboy would be proud to have as a centerfold, welcome to the graveyard shift." laughed Japes.

The night shift turned out to be quite an education, and he became rather enamored with Judy the hooker, sexy and provocative, she had a certain aura about her. He thought she looked special and apparently after cashing all those traveler checks he was not the only one. The cabbies started to call him "Ayah". Japes gave in one night and asked them why? They told Japes he had an eastern accent and he acted like a wombat. One could assume they intended flattery, like most players in the service world he had gotten labeled. Becoming popular with all the creatures involved in the night culture fueled his career interests.

Another part of the graveyard shift, which included the Flathead servers, involved auditing whereby they performed all the basic accounting functions for the daily Income journal. One accountant hailed from "Big Sky Country". Her name was Lily and, like his father would say, she had very good posture. She possessed a wide round face with a huge smile and short black hair cut straight as if she had a bowl on her head. Like most Flatheads she remained reserved at all times. The top accountant, Gertrude, a local girl exemplified all the typical Flathead features, and appeared quite unattractive wearing glasses as thick as the windshield of a car with a complexion reminiscent of the wicked witch of the east. All in all though the bean counters were a pleasure to work with. For the most part they stayed in the back and criticized all the bookkeeping mistakes the desk clerks made during the day. One could say they were the brains of the operation, as they carried out their duties and kept track of all the beans. As Japes became more and more popular with the staff the Flatheads wanted to participate. Connecting the Flatheads from the night world with the day crew honed his skills as a liaison. Inviting him to breakfast every morning, which for them was a dinner, bonded them while enjoying the usual eggs and of course a Bloody Mary. The best spot for this rendezvous occurred at the HoJo's directly across the street, located in just the right area whereby the night dwellers could sip on their cocktails and eat their scrambled eggs while enjoying the incredible vista. Conversations would start with something that occurred during the shift, but over a period of time became more personal in nature. The Montana girl would describe her hometown, and the differences in lifestyle as compared to where they now lived. The local girl would give the inside scoop on the area eateries and hidden watering holes. The breakfast club evolved into both a relaxing as well as an educational event. Always important for him to maintain a good relationship with everybody he worked with, he actively listened and learned. Having a good rapport with the staff

17

was as important as taking care of the guest. It all blended together and was something he had experienced in his youth.

Japes became attached to the "lords of the night" in a way that siblings' help one another, or a coach helps an athlete excel, it became the essence of finding balance.

THE STAGE

The night shift was now the new domain and he grew determined to make his mark. Several exciting interactions with a host of celebrities thrilled him to the core. Hailing from a small rural community where the only exposure to a celebrity stemmed from television or at the movies only compounded the anticipation of these luminary interactions. The first exciting moment occurred when he greeted Governor Ronald Reagan in the late 70's while he was campaigning for president. Although not politically inclined, the sheer enormity of the moment proved exciting, a simple hello and a smile entailed the extent of their meeting.

The hotel, located close to a comedy club, frequently hosted a number of national comedians. The celebrity you see on television is not always the one you deal with in person. Dom DeLuise delighted everyone when checking in, as he would oftentimes practice one of his routines on new desk clerks all just for fun. One of the regular guests, Joan Rivers, traveled with a large entourage wherever she went. Everyone wanted her time as she stood at the peak of her career. She could not have been nicer to every server in the hotel, and exceptionally appreciative for all the services she and her group required. Tony Bennet, also a true gentleman, appeared rather reserved for a famous singer and toured with a small crowd. The security department enlightened

Japes as to why he appeared so mellow. Apparently, his guest room suite was filled with a distinct aroma.

These cinema stars, although blessed with acting and comedic skills, were not much different from the average Joe. They were nice, they were rude, they were stoned, they were happy and they were sad. This displayed nothing that you did not observe in everyday life.

As soon as he arrived one evening Japes was welcomed by Gary the assistant front office manager. Gary represented a rare breed that one would occasionally run into during their career. A normal person surrounded by and in constant involvement with the not so normal. A well educated, well-spoken man from the Badlands region, who held no specific roots in the area. A tall, thin man who wore glasses, and who constantly kept track of everyone and everything in this chaotic world. Gary informed Japes that night, of a large group which had been pinned out of the top floor stemming from credit issues, meaning that a number of rooms were locked shut so that the guests could not reenter their guest rooms. Someone would be required to come to the desk and establish credit for the stay. Gary did not inform Japes whom it concerned or any circumstances surrounding the pin out. At three AM a heavyset bearded patron approached the desk. He mumbled, "Hey man we need our stuff, let us in our rooms." After checking out the room numbers he explained the situation to the bearded wonder.

The naivety to the situation played in his favor, as he had no idea the enormity of this celebrity's reputation. The patron pulled out a fistful of hundred dollar bills all crumbled and in complete disarray. He threw them all over the front desk in front of Japes. He then produced a dirty orange and white Mastercard, which he reluctantly slid across the desk. The man became impatient and kept repeating, "Hey man we need our stuff." The card was approved and along with the cash there would be enough money to open the rooms. This ended a rather odd evening.

First thing in the morning Mr. Rosh stopped him on his way to the time clock shook his hand and said great job. Bewildered, he asked what was all the fuss about. The staff had pinned out many rooms during his first few months in the hotel world with little fan fair. Mr. Rosh explained that the man was Jerry Garcia one of the Grateful Dead and that they were notorious for very slow payment of their bills all across the country. The hotel sales staff, so enamored with the group's stardom, never bothered to check their credit and thought they would simply send them a bill. The event marked a real victory for him on his way up the ladder.

A few weeks later the front office and in particular Gary were treated to what could best be described as a display of showmanship. A wealthy Arabic man had registered at the hotel and he along with his entourage occupied ten guest rooms. Mr. Asifyou kept extending his

21

stay, but at a certain point it became a serious issue. The hotel was oversold and Gary artfully persuaded the gentleman to leave, or so they thought. Finally, after a heated telephone conversation, the man reluctantly bellied up to the desk in full Arabic garb, which included his kaffiyeh and dish dash. He sauntered over to the cashier and settled his bill. Mr. Asifyou then proceeded to hand each desk clerk a crisp new one hundred dollar bill accompanied by a deep long bow of appreciation. Last, he approached Gary looked him up and down and from under his dish dash presented him with a banana and the accompanying bow. He and his entourage proceeded out the front door never to be seen again. Not to be outdone, Gary immediately ate the banana in full view of everyone and returned the deep bow.

Japes, preoccupied with his career, unknowingly became somewhat oblivious to his peers. Everyone was not interested in a career, and only after years had passed and he reflected on his first position did he understand what had transpired. In retrospect, one coworker in particular caught all the server's eyes. A rural server like Japes, she relocated from the Midland Region. She embodied beauty, standing five foot seven with a classic thirty-six twenty-four thirty-six hourglass figure. Peavy turned the heads of anyone she passed with her long wavy blonde hair and natural look. Peavy appeared older than she was with a robust figure not dissimilar to a famous movie star. She worked primarily on the day shifts from seven to three, but occasionally would work the evening shift from three to eleven. At some point, one of the sports teams checked into the hotel. They were called "The Los Angeles Lakers "and were the reigning champions of the world. Well low and behold Peavy was asked out on a dinner date with one of the most famous athlete coaches of all time, Jerry West. Peavy confided in all of the servers and told them there was no romance just a great dinner. Fortunate for her, as he was at least twice her age, and if looking for a husband had been on her mind, she needed to search elsewhere.

Her next adventure involved comedy legend Bill Cosby. Performing nightly at the club down the street, he broke all the rules and secretly invited her to the show. A charming man with a wonderful smile and great stories, he was also at least twice her age. Again, there had been no romance just a night of fun. Peavy dined on a petite filet mignon for dinner while he consumed three chilli dogs. She watched the show and laughed so hard she started to cry. She was no fool, why not accept the company of these famous people and enjoy the night, amazingly fantastic fuel for the evolving hotel gossip. It was forbidden by the company for anyone to see or talk to a guest outside of work, but nobody would ever tell. Japes learned early on that the rules were rules, but to never be a rat. Nobody would ever be so malicious as to drop a dime on Peavy. To ingratiate

23

oneself with one's supervisors by betraying a friend was a political lesson seen time and time again throughout his career. In fact many servers made and kept their careers with such behavior. He hated this more than anything, as these actions had no real bearing on the work at hand.

Another server who worked at the desk, named Kenner, hailed from the "Windy City" in the Midland Region of the country. Attractive, standing maybe five feet tall a hundred and ten pounds, she was a real dynamo. She presented herself as a real life Barbie Doll with red lipstick and a crinkled up nose. Kenner conveyed a wild girl's attitude constantly on the prowl. Japes remembered standing in the back hall adjacent to the cashier's room. There stood a long counter where everyone gathered and read the schedules and memos for the upcoming week. He stood there one day with his hands holding onto the counter while Kenner slipped up next to him and with the gentlest of hip checks whispered lets go get them big guy. She looked at him, winked and went on her merry way to the front desk. Japes did not have a clue and although he turned red as a beet he did nothing. Luckily he did not jump into any relationship with Kenner, as Kenner shortly thereafter ended up with Sonny the young handsome manager from the front desk. A management trainee from the "City of Cars", he had recently achieved a master's degree and appeared ready to conquer the world. A high-energy server who dressed in expensive suits and always looked the part. Hitting the floor one night and commencing to perform rapid pushups behind the front desk, placed Sonny into a rarely observed category. Geared up about walking patrons, he became compelled to relieve the stress, so he thought exercise would help. It did not, and the night crew laughed so hard they started to cry as they eventually relocated the guests. Crinkle nose and Sonny made a pretty darn good couple, and the scuttlebutt exploded as they were purportedly seen skinny-dipping together at Sonny's condominium in the clubhouse pool. The rumor mill in the server world continued to evolve.

Bobo, another character that Japes worked with at the front desk, was a handsome thirty six-year-old from the Badlands Region who reminded one of Tom Sellick. Rather old to be a desk clerk, he epitomized true server skills and displayed exceptional talent. Bobo stood tall with broad shoulders and an old soul. He knew his limitations and could not handle the stress of managing, as he would become flustered over some rather mundane and typical situations. Nonetheless, he enjoyed what he did and was fun to be around.

They became great friends and played numerous rounds of golf together on their days off from the hotel. Bobo played everything with a heavy draw and aimed 20 yards to the right of his target. A burly man, he managed to come over the top with amazing consistency, and truly thumped the ball. The misses, however, were equally as dramatic and required him to maintain a steady inventory of golf balls. Japes, on the other hand, slightly built, relied on a combination of rhythm and technique to navigate the links. The two enjoyed the 19th hole with plenty of beer and always a steak dinner. Bobo thrived as a professional desk clerk naturally projecting instant understanding to the weary traveler. The ability to instantly bring a corporate guest into a reassuring, professional, and secure environment highlighted an innate gift. If one met Bobo at a cocktail party they would become engaged in comfortable conversation thinking he was a professional of some sort. That is exactly what he was, and indeed one of the best.

His dad was an oil executive with More-money Inc. and so he never wanted for anything. Bobo lived well beyond the means of a desk clerk. There was nothing wrong with this, and in some ways it seemed quite appropriate. Hotels tend to attract people from all walks of life and require a myriad of special skills not readily recognized or appreciated, so if someone could survive and fulfill this calling then the more the merrier. He met a few servers in his career just like Bobo. Everyone had their niche and for Japes it became evident that the great majority of his fellow servers, whether they were a line person, a manager, or an executive could not be labeled. Those who were, fit neatly into a provocative category reserved for takers.

Winter came to the mountains and Japes went skiing with Sonny and Kenner. He could not remember exactly how but Peavy became the fourth in their group. This was not a date, but somebody was trying to hook them up. Sonny drove and of course he owned a sports car that came right off the showroom floor. He and Kenner were both outfitted with top-of-the-line ski apparel, equipment, and dressed in the best of everything. Japes had not skied for years, so he borrowed his brother's skis and boots. He found a hat that used to be his sisters, and a warm parka, but the outfit did not match. Sonny and Kenner were excellent skiers, and the truth would be revealed only when they all traversed the snowy slopes. Now there were two certainties about Japes that few knew. One, he was born with server-dystrophy and although not discernible it did affect his physical strength. He carried a different appearance that nobody could quite put a finger on, as he looked like a skinny baseball pitcher with rounded shoulders. The other facts about Japes were if he said he could do something he could do it, as well as always knowing his limits, lessons well learned in his youth.

The group ended up at the Head-spin Resort in the Mountain Region about two hours outside of the city. He learned how to ski back east on smaller mountains under more difficult icy conditions when he was just seven years old. On the first run, once everyone loosened up, Sonny and Kenner displayed their downhill expertise. Peavy made no

27

such claims to be an expert, and she simply enjoyed the day, as she carefully maneuvered down all of the trails at her own steady pace. The amount and fluffy nature of the snow out west brought a smile to Japes face, as he could not believe how great the conditions were. He went down the slopes with the greatest of ease and stopped on a dime grinning from ear to ear. The other three looked on in amazement, as he had not been bragging or selling himself, he just did what he could do. All in all a fun day and another lesson remembered from his father. " We are what we do, not what we say we do!" The group celebrated with a glorious feast that night joined by some of the other hotel servers. Back in the city, he gave Peavy a ride home to her apartment, but alas there would be no romance. That perhaps was a mistake as she was a real sweet server who got away.

The Transition

Japes had been to a number of social gatherings with his peers as he neared his one-year anniversary. Mary, the lobby bartender, had tried to seduce him at the bosses' house. She was older, in her late twenties, and had been around the block a few times. A blonde haired middle-aged party girl who reminded him that one can do wonders with some makeup and lipstick. Most of the night evolved around her sitting on his lap as if they had known each other for years. Letting this server go home alone proved a wise decision, as he wanted to learn all he could and maintain his interest in a career. Confused about combining the two, he wisely focused on his inherent passion to serve.

In the hotel world, there is a plethora of subcultures loosely connected to each other, therfore in one that employs six hundred staff servers a move up to management would immediately change one's status, and would be an important career step. On the practical side, he earned only two hundred dollars per week, which would make it difficult to survive. His desire for advancement was conveyed to Mr. Rosh and to Mr. Cribs, along with a Regional Bull who helped place managers in the company. He knew Sonny, placed as a management trainee, was "on the move", likewise he thought for sure management would promote him up the ladder, after all, he collected money from notorious groups, had walked hundreds of guests without a complaint, demonstrated outstanding cashiering accuracy for thousands and thousands of dollars, and gained a high status within the front office group.

The brass told him that he needed a little more time that he didn't "look the part". He didn't stand up straight enough and he did not fit his suit properly. He looked kind of skinny and needed to develop a little bit more. Discrimination at any level is humiliating! A real tough pill to swallow since Mother Nature herself could not make him stand up any straighter. After about three minutes of reflection, he told management to stuff it. Deciding to leave along with his friend Bobo and the desk manager to search out a new world in the Midland Region proved fruitful. Obviously this world was not a meritocracy, but that did not mean one could not be found.

He should have been bitter and mad, but he was not that surprised. What other servers thought of him was of no real consequence, only what he thought of himself truly mattered. He loved Mr. Rosh the massive General Manager who drove the old Chevy II station wagon full of empty beer cans; who watched pornographic movies on "Spankvision" in his office, as part of his guest entertainment evaluation process. He loved Judy the hooker who turned three tricks a night, and the half-shaven cabbie named Tom who called him ayah. He reflected in the interactions around the desk clerks who he worked with. Remembering Charlie, the acne faced millionaire who like Bobo was a professional desk clerk brought a smile to his face. They all had interesting stories and interesting lives outside of the profession. Japes recalled the morning he worked alone with three hundred and fifty checkouts and the seven to three shift ran late. There stood fifty guests waiting in line and he persevered the best he could. Unaware halfway down the line his favorite athlete of all time slowly moved toward him. Japes looked up, smiled, and said "Hondo Havlicek!" The great basketball star smiled back and shook his hand. What a world this young server had landed in, with literally thousands of meetings and brief discussions as guests came and went. Japes did not care what the brass proclaimed he knew he was ready to move on and it was just a matter of where.

Bobo and Japes drove to the "Wind City" and another Marion Hotel. Their friend Gary, from the Mountain Region, recently moved there so they decided to visit and see what was up. They crashed at Bobo's sisters, who taught at Northwestern University, and proceeded to check out the hotel sites. Gary worked on trying to persuade them to stay, but Japes decided to take a chance traveling to a new stage and a new career. He journeyed to a different city and plunged into a drastically different world. That would be the last time he ever saw or spoke to Bobo and Gary, and like many who pursue a life as a server searching for the "best home" one was forced to move. Unfortunately, this transient

31

lifestyle made it difficult to maintain lifelong relationships and for Japes it presented a true negative.

HOME

Japes reflected on his childhood as he enjoyed a one-week trip across the country to his newest adventure. Visiting areas of interest while he meandered his way across the country brought a smile to his face. Away from home for one year flew by like a lightning bolt, yet so much had already happened. He grew up on a two hundred acre spread in an enormous old farmhouse. The main house included a library, eight bedrooms, two dining rooms, two living areas, a pantry, and an eat-in kitchen. A great place to play games during those long, cold northern winters, he never felt confined. The family owned a mile of lake frontage, which included two beaches, a sandbar, a cranberry bog, and numerous docks for diving and boating. A playground fit for a prince where most children could grow up enjoying a satisfying life, knowing all they wanted would evolve around being healthy and happy. Understanding he would need something special to match his early years, he emerged an idealist. Having been born into a fitting environment within a beautiful setting, proved simply breathtaking. The resort, situated adjacent to a lake filled with crystal clear water, featured a view of the mountains, cascading to the foothills, all being reflected in the shimmering surf. The pure air and the forever peaceful silence defined his savoir-faire.

As far back as he could remember, his parents were always at home, as they managed the hotel every summer while entertaining up to fifty patrons at a time. Guests enjoyed breakfast, lunch, and dinner, in the dining room, and occupied their own pine- paneled cabin complete with all the facilities including a fireplace. Japes loved his job of being the water boy delivering bottles of spring water, taken from the well at the top of the hill, and a bucket of ice to each cabin. The tap water contained chlorine, and the guests would never dream of consuming such a poor offering. Welcomed like a conquering hero, Japes, delivered the water, thus marking the start of the cocktail hour for all the patrons as they savored pure, clean well water and ice for their drinks. The guests also enjoyed swimming, fishing, canoeing, hiking, golf, reading, card games, blueberry picking, and of course the conversation.

Japes grew up in a resort and met every type of person known to mankind or so he thought. Anyone who could afford a summer vacation at a beautiful resort frequented this area. In the off-season his real friends were the locals. Japes, in reality, embodied the identity of a "local" he simply enjoyed the benefit of having the world come to him every summer. A community of five hundred, growing to five thousand during "the season", along with his friends and parents would bestow upon him his values.

Pete, Japes father, a tall, slender man with a long nose and a year-round tan always had a Camel cigarette hanging out of the left side of his mouth. Stoic and thoughtful, he loved the great outdoors and all that nature could bring, he taught his children how to hunt and fish and appreciate nature. Pete and Japes similarity ran deeper than father and son they both inherited server-dystrophy causing physical restrictions affecting their ability to move like the others, and inevitably played a role in defining their lives. Pete taught him that everyone had strengths and weaknesses most of which one could not see with the eye. Since the two of them appreciated life with certain limitations their other gifts and interests more than offset the obvious shortfall. Fate provides a way of balancing and sometimes even remarkable accomplishments can occur. The locals called them Pete and Re-Pete, he surmised this to be a sign of affection.

From here he learned his life lessons. Pete taught him not to care what others thought of him, but to always respect their views. "You may be right, you may be wrong, but you will always be you." Pete often stated, "It's not what people say that matters, it's what they do." Although Pete was not an authoritative figure he held fast to these two beliefs. He knew there were many non-believers in the world, but one could always hope. Some might say that this was not much of a foundation, but it would turn out to be just enough. These beliefs were tested many times as he grew.

The resort, absolutely stunning, with a pristine majestic piece of land surrounded by mountains and a lake perched on a Fairview Hill, attracted families for generations. The rolling fields speckled with apple and pear trees gave way to the mountain views. You name it Japes did it from flying a kite to shooting clay pigeons. Every experience presented to him was well received, and each day presented a new adventure filling him with the desire to never leave. Why would anyone want to venture out when everything one needed was right there?

Japes gift, his sense of humor, carried him through thick and thin with well-timed laughter. Anybody with a sense of humor quickly related, and so he never trusted anyone who couldn't or wouldn't laugh. Pete sometimes would laugh so hard he would start to cry. At the hotel's cocktail hour his parents occasionally disclosed stories about their children. On one such occasion they revealed one involving Japes. One summer Bishop Mulligan employed Japes to cut some trees and do general yard work. Despite the great difference in age, George sixty-five and Japes fourteen, the two developed a good friendship. George hailed from the Midland Region and spent his summers enjoying Vacationland. Playing many memorable rounds of golf together, this is where Japes learned people of the cloth do swear! One day George told him they were going to build a martin house, "A what kind of house," he asked, "A martin house," said George, "it is a type of bird." Well, they erected the structure, but it proved to be quite difficult. It required a twelve-foot pole, with a large birdhouse on top, to be sunk deep down into the earth. Japes dug rocks and roots out of the ground for hours to secure the pole. When all was said and done, he received his five dollars for the day. The bishop was definitely not a big spender. He asked him "What do you think?" Japes looked up and down the pole and replied, "Best damn martin house I ever built".

And so it went, he met with and played with all sorts of people every summer. In the fall, he learned how to hunt. In the winter he learned how to ski. In the spring he was in heaven. He and his brother would fish from dawn till dusk.

The hotel and Japes home were one and the same. Business to him appeared the same as having a big family. Although the family business lasted only a few months, the home remained year-round. This reality brought perspective to his life, where in the same kitchen, Japes could be doing the dishes for fifty guests or his family's dinner. The same task under completely different circumstances instilled a feeling of relaxation. He felt comfortable in hotels as they always reminded him of home. This next trip would challenge his teachings, as he was not going to a hotel he was going to an institution. Journeying off for money, and the security of working with family opened a new door.

GRUBLAND

Japes, presented with an opportunity through his family to work in the world of grub, seized the moment. His uncle, UJ, president of the largest grub service in the world, embodied a true Bull with a big round face and a body to match, reminding anyone of Santa Claus. UJ enjoyed his teenage years working with Japes father at their family resort. A self-made millionaire, working in every management position on his way up the corporate ladder became a gifted provider of grub. A remarkable story of success and determination that eventually bestowed upon him the nickname "King of Grub." During the days leading up to his start date Japes navigated his way through a series of courtesy interviews, his uncle wanted no one in the company to be aware of his nephew. Even the district manager, kept in the dark, would offer no preferential treatment, for moving up the ladder on his own merit just like his uncle required stealth and commitment.

Grubland and the world within dramatically differed from the hotels Japes grew so familiar with. The facility fed five thousand students every day for breakfast, lunch, and dinner. The kitchen alone employed over two hundred, while the entire facility engaged three hundred and fifty employees. A virtual feeding factory, and as assistant manager, he inherited the responsibility of opening the kitchen at five AM every morning. Supervising the cashiers, the runners, and whatever other front of the house staffing required to feed the masses, held his time. He, however, liked and hung out with the cooks more than any of the other servers, and he learned much from them.

Kitty, his boss, and the unit manager, appeared as an attractive server, a little older than Japes and an Influencer. Her hair, dark and straight, looking focused and professional at all times, Kitty displayed the appearance of a doctor or a dentist as she always wore a white smock in the kitchen. Her boss Mohan, the district manager, twenty years her senior, represented a boisterous, handsome man with dark curly hair, always immaculately attired, who unknowingly created an intense culture. Mohan coincidentally worked in the same building, and also happened to be Kitty's husband. The scuttlebutt climaxed with the universal opinion, it appeared a pity for Kitty to have hooked up with such an older man. Nobody could quite figure out why the two married, residing in an enormous old colonial in a ritzy neighborhood not far from work. Spending money like it grew on trees, constantly venturing to restaurants, clubs, and various social engagements consumed their personal life. Mohan was "the man", but everyone knew Kitty ran the show. On a number of stressful occasions Mohan became so overwhelmed that he either broke down in tears or screamed at the top of his lungs to whomever or whatever set him off. Stability avoided his professional makeup.

This represented another world, and another business, but fortunately there were many givers hidden in the crowd. The magnitude of the facility proved greater than anything he had ever seen. When running at full capacity the crew working in the kitchen toiled nonstop, as feeding five thousand students took an energetic, enormous staff, and an incredible amount of food. Japes did not know it then, but he would taste literally every food item in existence in one form or another during his tenure. Opening the building proved an important task and he arrived at the loading dock every morning at five AM. It would be catastrophic if he were late for breakfast, as nobody wanted five thousand hungry students stampeding the entryway. Japes recalled only one opening debacle on an early spring morning when showing up bright and early to open the doors. Sometimes Henry, the receiver, arrived before him, a wonderful server who once boxed professionally, possessed an average build, and owned the softest hands and gentlest touch of any person he ever met. Nobody realized that this server, once a golden gloves champion who could take you out with one quick punch, had sadly been relegated to the position of a receiver. Henry's smile lit up a room, and his laid back demeanor kept everyone relaxed. He told Japes stories of his boxing days, and some of his great fights, a gentleman with a disposition as far from the vicious reality of a true fighter that one could imagine. That day, as Japes walked up to the loading dock, there were dozens of boxes scattered on the floor containing the early pastry deliveries. In one box, a rat with a doughnut in its mouth peacefully chomped this newly discovered bounty. Sitting back on its haunches it appeared so large Japes believed it to be a cat. He informed Kitty of the situation and she asked "how many did he get" Japes replied "he ate just one." "Okay." she replied, "what's the question". Should I throw out the pastries the rat could have walked through all the boxes? "OH NO! " She replied. "There are rats everywhere we would never get a meal out if we did that." Wow, thought Japes, this is some kind of a world. Cleanliness is next to godliness, but in this case it appeared next to impossible.

Japes, one of the few white servers working at the facility, raised to not be prejudice became intrigued with the new culture and their ways. Becoming both speculative and open-minded in his observation over the next few months he came to the conclusion that they were in no way different from the people he grew up with. A new lesson learned and kept to this day. For some reason he was labeled "John the Baptist", though it made no sense it stuck. He figured once you are labeled, it showed a certain level of acceptance, as well as an initial measure of respect and trust for the young manager.

The routine for the manager remained basic, after the loading dock opened and making sure everyone arrived at their' post, the mad rush commenced. The cooks prepared their stations and fired up the grills, while the salad ladies chopped lettuce and boiled eggs. The runners filled ice bins and placed food items on the lines, simultaneously brewing enormous quantities of coffee. Bagels and toast were all started in multi-slotted toasters, when the doors opened and thousands of students passed through the cafeteria. This all happened within a six-hour period. At seven AM the mad rush would commence and slowly subside by one PM. He had never seen so many students and so much food consumed in such a short period of time. Although Japes graduated from college, this job would turn out to be quite an education. Massive productions in the world of grub were not unusual, but the scope and volume at Grubland were unparalleled. This hard physical work required a tremendous labor force trained to handle organized chaos. The staff, both nice and hard working were limited in their abilities and appeared destined to pursue this endeavor for the rest of their lives. It presented an experience distant from the hotel culture.

Mayo, the only full-time busboy, tall, slender, and always punctual, was quite a character. A black server with a scruffy appearance and a quasi-Van Dyke goatee, Japes figured he inherited some sort of learning disability as he grinned and mumbled to himself all day long. Everyone made exceptions for Mayo thus allowing him to be part of the team. Through years of repetition, he developed a thorough understanding of his well-established routine. One of Japes first managerial challenges, per Kitty, involved teaching Mayo how to properly shave even though he was a fifty-year old server not some wayward teenager. Mayo always looked half shaven with his whiskers a flying, as he had worked there for twenty years and nobody ever encouraged him to change anything. It took all of his skills to persuade Mayo as to the virtues of a nice clean look, and eventually he took it to heart by shaving very close. When Mayo arrived at work he looked as though he shaved with a lawnmower with his face cut in many places and he, rightfully agitated. Japes learned, after the fact, that many black men have curly facial hair, which can be difficult to groom. He could not have felt worse about his failure both to Mayo and to his boss. He apologized to Mayo and told him to shower every day, but to groom any way he wanted. He told his boss, despite her insistence that everyone be clean-shaven, that Mayo was not going to change his appearance. "Servers are all a little different." Japes said, and he'd be damned if he was going to embarrass and humiliate anyone for some ridiculous directive. The boss was not always right, in fact, he wondered if they were ever correct.

He landed in a different world, and he soon realized this institution required a strong back and an uncertain mind to make a living. All the workers were of limited skills and the daily tasks were enormous. The dishwashing crew seemed to be highly organized and efficient. They all emigrated from the Subcontinent and only one spoke English. Their area always looked spotless and they never appeared bored. The group, featuring an equal number of men and women performed the same job, humming a melodious chant, which permeated the kitchen with a soothing and pleasant tempo. He felt uncertain, but maybe this ratio had something to do with their great harmony. Slinger, the one and only pots and pans guy, performed a little different than the other servers, as he stood isolated at the pot sink. There was not a tremendous future in being a pot washer, but Slinger enjoyed a secret skill, he liked to weld. This may have been something he learned in his home country nobody really knew, but Slinger's hobby of welding all kinds of metal, including pots and pans, into works of art occasionally showed up at work. The craftsmanship amazed everyone, as he creatively made a large pot look like a mountain with stone faces and trees. All of his work appeared unique and, with a little help from everyone, his creations were displayed in a gallery. This highlighted a great moment for Slinger, and although he never realized any real money from his passion, he gifted his work to the multitude.

The main cafeteria, which Japes looked after, consisted of a large group of older servers. The cashiers were older women, many of whom were grandmothers, they treated him like a son and were a pleasure to work with. He remained single so the ladies were constantly attempting to hook him up with one of the coeds. Two servers who worked for Grubland were "local girls". They were colorful and liked to party. Many of the servers would gather at a local watering hole every Friday night to drink and tell stories. Japes, labeled the new guy by the girls, after a few weeks received an invitation. Dumb and Dumber were street wise and fast-paced. After one drink, and just meeting Dumb for the first time she looked at him and started patting herself. She hurriedly patted her lap in a circular motion all the time giggling, and playing to the crowd. "Japes, what am I doing?" asked Dumb. "I have no idea," said Japes. "I am beating around the bush" she replied, quite an introduction from a complete stranger. And so this exposed part of the new world Japes had landed in. Hanging with these girls most definitely put a chill down his spine, and in fact the servers who befriended him the most turned out to be the black servers.

He knew what it felt like to be discriminated against, as his unusually narrow build and sunken chest became the object of ridicule throughout his youth. Well-honed psychological lines of defense had been fully developed by this point in his life, and certainly his new friends could relate. Appreciating his company, and accepting him into the culture, this new group, both from local communities and from other countries became his ally. Some had even been in prison for serious crimes, but what struck him the most, since this was the first time he worked with this group, was their sincerity. Coming from vastly different backgrounds with enormous education and life opportunity distinctions, could not have been wider. Despite that, they all realized he was a straight shooter, and that he appreciated their hard work, loyalty, and inner beauty, particularly the ladies from the islands. Dressed up to the nines and looking great, they would go clubbing every Friday night. They displayed no pretense, Japes admired and respected their lives, and in return he received sincerity, not rhetoric.

Luster, the "production server", oversaw the entire kitchen, which meant stress surrounded him, as it certainly was not easy to produce five thousand meals every single day. He appeared half Irish and half Chinese, looking like a fishing bobber with the top half cut at an angle. Short and heavy, constantly bossing everyone around while patrolling his territory, his cooking and ordering of food represented his two claims to fame, as Luster showed no interest in building, or for that matter recognizing, relationships. Perhaps this behavior related to his upbringing or maybe his personal circumstances, but it separated him from the crowd. He did, however, work well with the Executive Chef Bob to keep things rolling. Luster had serious personal issues with his family, so Japes learned to give him a wide birth. He acted, however, the antithesis of the black servers, as he was insincere, unfaithful, prejudice, and difficult to approach. Hitting on the coeds even though married with two young children developed into a habit. Go figure, he turned out to be a successful manager, which spoke volumes about this particular culture.

Bob, the Executive Chef, a former Navy man exemplified a true Racer. A tall, thin, man always working, reminding everyone of Gomer Pyle with a thinner nose and a grayish color to his skin, for no particular reason befriended Japes. One day Japes noticed a half empty bottle of whiskey by one of the grills. He asked Bob, "What recipe called for whiskey?" Bob replied "My recipe," as he gulped a full swig out of a paper cup. "Old-school" said Bob, "It smooth's out the day." No wonder he shown such a gray complexion, he was half in the wrapper 24 hours a day. They want everybody clean shaving yet drinking while you were working somehow complied with the standards.

After a few months on the job, the corporate chef arrived for a quarterly visit. Reviewing all the recipes for the entire company and taste testing encompassed most of his day. He wrote award winning cookbooks and prepared meals for a countless number of dignitaries including the

President of The United States. A gifted chef and well respected throughout the grub industry Luigi epitomized the ultimate Bull weighing in somewhere north of four hundred pounds. Barking like a junkyard dog with the sophisticated look of Burl Ives enabled Luigi to intimidate the entire staff. So large that one day when he had fallen, it took three servers to help him stand up again. Oh man, could he eat, as Luigi not only tasted everything that he cooked, he also ate enormous portions becoming a proverbial eating machine.

Luigi treated everybody like dirt and Japes was no exception, if anything, he treated him worse, being new to the kitchen and easy to bully. When testing recipes, Luigi directed Japes all over the kitchen to gather ingredients, continuously making him shell shrimp or chop vegetables just to show he ruled the roost. "Dice the vegetables on a slant, and I want them exactly the same size. Then devein the shrimp like this. Let's go." Luigi barked "Why like that?" asked Japes. "Just do it and do it fast," snorted the overweight bully. He acted like a dog marking around his territory, so nobody would enter. Many of the servers loved getting Luigi's dander up, in particular, the salad ladies always leaped about right in front of him, hoping he would tip over as he looked like a fish out of water flopping on the floor. The loud and boisterous inevitably were compensating for some unknown shortcoming.

After a Christmas break, when all the servers enjoyed some time off, they returned to work. Luigi discovered that Japes was the company president's nephew who just happened to be Luigi's boss. Japes, unaware of this revelation, became truly shocked when Luigi started treating him with respect. He went out of his way to show him cooking techniques and various tricks of the trade. Japes initiation into the corporate world of politics felt like a light turning on in his head, Luigi simply wanted to stay on his uncle's good graces, it had nothing to do with actually being civil.

Another part of Grubland, which opened every day for lunch called the Back Street Pub offered beer and wine. The hot food line served burgers, hot dogs, and French fries, and was staffed entirely with black servers. Beverly, the manager, an island server with a great personality, a beautiful round face, and a perfect ebony complexion oversaw the show. She and Japes were true soul mates seeing life through the same hospitality prism. Often times he would open up the pub for Beverly, as she inevitably would stay until last call.

One afternoon, everyone was running behind, and Japes appeared stressed. Neville, a former convict, the only cook at his station remained steadfast and cool, as both he and Japes realized they were in a predicament. The pub needed to be open in just fifteen minutes and they were under the gun. The other cook, Mike, arrived late, Japes asked him if he needed help setting up his station. Mike gave him a blank look and started to turn on his grills. Mike, a young server who never said too much, appeared to be reliable and rather likable. Japes hollered to Neville and Mike "Oh boy, we need to move fast!" The pub doors were about to open, and the crowd would be rushing in. Mike suddenly leaped over the counter with a ten-inch French knife and pushed him up against the wall. "Who the hell are you calling a boy!" yelled Mike. Japes, petrified, slowly caught his breath as Neville took Mike's arm and pulled him back. Neville said, "He did not call anyone boy it was just an expression". Incensed by this misunderstanding, Mike nearly cut Japes with an uncontrollable urge to strike out. Neville saved him from some serious injury and thought nothing of it; he regularly drank with Japes and the gang on Friday nights, and knew Japes was not a bigot. His bosses blew off the incident as if nothing occurred, thinking he made it out to be much more than a simple misunderstanding. This world steadily filled with muddy waters, when serious issues were not even discussed and trivial details became important. Hopefully, all of management was not like this or his time in Grubland would be quite short.

"Hey, what are you doing with that yellow tape?" asked Japes. "Who are you?" " I am with the FDA son, and I am shutting down this entire facility. This storage room is full

of dead rats, and the walls are crawling with cockroaches."
This distinguished looking man meant business and Japes
leaped to Kitty's office to inform her. "Oh Dam!" exclaimed
Kitty. "We need to buy forty eight hours or we will all lose our
jobs". Somehow, she obtained a delay and the FDA would
inspect again in two days. Everything was immediately taken
off the floors, and all areas including the walls and ceilings
thoroughly sanitized, simultaneously, drilling holes behind
stainless steel cabinets to eradicate the cockroaches.
Treating these areas with strong chemicals every night
revealed hundreds and hundreds of dead cockroaches each
morning. This unending battle never missed a beat during
his tenure in the land of Grub.

"They will never understand us, " said Ralph, the
enormous rat. He was the one Japes had seen eating a
doughnut. Chatting with Ralph early in the morning as he
licked up spilled beer at his favorite spot behind the bar
when no one occupied the pub somehow seemed normal.
"What are they not able to understand?" Asked Japes. " We
are not like humans, we just want to survive. Rats are not
dirty Grubland is dirty." "But Ralph you carry germs all over
and contaminate everything you touch." "Not true," snapped
Ralph. "We eat bugs and critters that would take over your
world. We keep you safe and for thanks you set traps and
poison." Japes suddenly awoke from the sound of a fire

52

engine and realized he had been dreaming about the day's events.

His home, a studio apartment not far from his work, echoed the clinging and clanging of the trolley wheels constantly reminding Japes of his less than desirable apartment location. Living in a shaky neighborhood, only a few hundred yards from the 'night life', and being the only white person in the building gave him reason to wonder. His family asked," What makes you think it is not a safe area?" " It is suggested that I secure a six foot long crow bar up against the door as a lock every night; this is not exactly The Ritz." That night, as Japes sat looking out at a five-alarm fire across the street, he decided to call home. "What kind of a place have I landed in?" He asked his mother. ""They are all different, but keep working hard, you will do fine," She stated. "Mom, I am sitting here with my feet up watching half of a city block go up in flames, and I live in an apartment that has a metal bar fastened to my door to keep me safe. My only true friends are from a different culture, yet somehow they are more like my childhood buddy's than any of the others. My boss does not worry about important things just what people think I'm confused." "Don't group your problems JP, especially when you don't really have any," said his mother. Japes loved his mother and knew all these questions would be answered with time, besides it was almost summer and he would be going away to a camp. Grubland closed for the summer and he would be assigned a cook's job at a camp for young girls, it would be a quick trip north to a little town in the country.

This camp for girls employed dozens of female counselors, and acquired the "hired help" from local laborers, mirroring many similar camps in the "Land of Conifers." This religion demanded specific requirements concerning its cuisine, and the chef could only prepare approved meals. The camp owner, Ms. Tender, a true mentsch, displaying an enormous honker of a nose, formally announced, "Now make sure you follow all the recipes and do not change a thing. Keep away from the girls at all times; your accommodations are over there." She pointed across the camp to a farmhouse with a sprawling front porch.

Japes and the staff of two were popular with everyone, and feeding two hundred proved insignificant in comparison to satisfying five thousand. The camp girls dined on lobsters and steaks for dinner, and feasted on fresh blueberry flapjacks or poached eggs for breakfast. It may have been a camp, but they ate better than if they were at home. Japes and the boys allocated most of their free time in three places. They drank beer on the porch of the farmhouse, they drank beer at the local gin mill named the Cracked Platter, or they went skinny dipping with the counselors.

The camp, however, would not allow the staff to swim if unable to complete a swim test, so Penny, one of the counselors, conducted the tests while the others watched. "Japes one final test requires you to complete the dead man's float for one full minute. Can you handle that?" asked Penny. "Sure" replied Japes, I am an accomplished swimmer. He lay prone, flat in the water extending his feet and arms parallel to the bottom of the lake unable to maintain his form he repeatedly failed. After a time, his head protruded from the murky depths to witness the entire gang laughing. "Come on Japes you can do it everyone else did." "What is so funny" Japes demanded. "Let your arms and legs hang down, 'Mr. Know it all,' that is the dead man's float." "Cooking and floating are your only requirements for enjoying the summer so get with it," laughed Penny, as everyone crashed cannonballs on him and suddenly scurried away for a beer.

All the servers enjoyed beer just some enjoyed it more than others, and at the Cracked Platter that night the gang rejoiced into the wee hours. To initiate the festivities everyone selected a partner and hit the dance floor, between laughing, telling stories, dancing, and consuming pitchers of beer the night flew by. Swimming in a nearby pond grew into a nightly ritual, to relax and close out the evening the servers participated in skinny-dipping with the light of the moon, with romance in the air and beer in the belly. Enjoying croaking like the real frogs and splashing with the girls, Japes asked Penny, "Why are there piles of green M&Ms on the kitchen stoop each morning?" "The young camp girls leave them for you, as they believe you are quite the gifted chef and the green M&Ms will bring you love." "What do you think Penny?" "It appears you need to practice your croaking back at the farmhouse." A -Yah " said Japes and they were off.

The summer unveiled a fun routine as Japes, the cooks, and the counselors fully appreciated the Vacationland experience. Simon, the downtrodden food manager, struggled to muster a smile and continuously downplayed the fun encounters. One day he challenged Japes to a contest of skill. Simon bragged of being a low handicap golfer and claimed he could hit a driver off the front porch of the farmhouse up the driveway at least two hundred and twenty yards. "Your saying the ball will fly or roll up the road without going off and hitting a tree?" Queried Tommy the cook. "Yes." replied Simon. "I will bet Japes a day off for everyone that I can hit it further up the road than he can before it goes into the woods." "Come on Japes what do you think." The road extended three or four hundred yards, surrounded by trees requiring one to hit a low shot down a virtual tunnel. Simon surmised he would put the entire gang in their place, and he would beat them down to prove he remained in charge. "Okay" said Japes, "Your up first." Simon hit a low bullet right off the porch, it nicked a tree on the left, but traveled to the bend in the road roughly one hundred and ninety yards before falling off. "Beat that " said Simon, "Do not let the gang down." Simon did not know that

Japes grew up near the camp, and that he played golf since the age of ten, he would have needed to actually establish a relationship with the staff to appreciate their lives. Japes dropped a ball on the porch and in one smooth motion ripped a low fade around the bend in the road the ball never left the drive and the crew took Sunday off. "You never told me you played golf," stated Simon. "You never asked." replied Japes.

Summer reached its inevitable conclusion and the campers traveled home, although Japes had fun, he knew this world and the Grubland world were not his cup of tea, the hotel environment lived in his blood, and it is where he always felt at peace. The size of his wallet proved less meaningful than the type of world he would choose. That summer he decided the culture undoubtedly held the vital component missing in his quest, so he started on another long trip, still without any true new friends or lasting relationships. This grub culture felt different, and it evolved into a series of chores. It was difficult but necessary to find a balance. Would it be possible to live a life similar to the one in " The Land of Conifers", or would he be destined to forever roam the country? Not excited about enduring a life as a nomad with numerous acquaintances and few friends, he knew, however, that he would thrive in a hotel, as the more opportunity he created to interact with those who truly served the greater his chances for success.

The Stepping Stone

A few days ago Japes fancied skinny-dipping in a pristine lake with beautiful girls, the Celtics defeated Houston for their 14th title, and today he interviewed for a position in the most spectacular hotel he had ever seen. The lobby area, designed to look like an open courtyard, anchored an atrium, which featured an award-winning bar and restaurant requiring reservations weeks in advance. Lush vegetation scattered throughout gave guests the feeling of being outdoors. The entire main floor, constructed of red brick imprinted with a floral design, established an eye-opening sense of arrival. Laboring every night, Mort the houseman, navigated a Zamboni-like machine for six hours to clean and polish every nook and cranny until the area shined like a diamond. In the morning light, with the floor glistening, one felt as though they were floating across rust colored lily pads. Looking up from the lobby, they observed five stories of guest room's, each room included a small balcony allowing guests to observe the activities below. Of all the views, the exterior facing rooms offered the most dramatic, with stunning vistas of the great divide. Japes quickly reconnected with the mountain city where his journey began.

The front desk itself, located to the side of the entrance, replicated a virtual island completely surrounded by public space; this unique design received regular compliments from travelers, as well as design awards from the building trade. Interviewing for a management position, he impressed someone being immediately hired as the new desk manager to supervise the shifts responsible for checking guests in and out of the hotel. He reported directly to the front office manager, who oversaw the entire department.

Mr. Suave, the general manager of the hotel, in no way appeared to be your typical hotel executive. "Good morning Japes, what is the house count today?" He would inquire in a deep voice. Asking the exact same question every day apparently meant money was his primary concern, although, looking quite distinguished with his shiny silver hair and dark complexion, he revealed little insight as to what type of server he represented.

After some time had passed, he observed Mr. Suave assisting a guest with their luggage, as he bent over Japes noticed a pistol hidden under his sports coat. What have I gotten myself into, thought Japes. Later he discovered, Mr. Suave once commanded an FBI task force and for protection he packed heat, furthermore, he not only held the general manager's position of this hotel, he also held a regional director's position, overseeing four other properties. His role within the organization proved to be greater than it first appeared. He also garnered a reputation with the ladies. Life felt different in this world, as everything appeared new and exciting at the Marion Hotel, here, duties and interactions with customers became refined. Maturing enough to take on new responsibilities, Japes, however, remained creative, instilling fun and humor into the endless change of day. The essence of hospitality encompassed multiple layers of pure fun to be shared by all.

Billy had been the part time night auditor who worked only one shift a week. He most assuredly was not a Flathead who represented the vast majority of these late night bean counters. Of average build with a round happy face and always dressed in a perfectly sized suit, Billy recently relocated from the east to make his mark. He spoke with no discernible accent, however, the gift of gab embedded in his DNA, propelled him to constant chatter.

"Japes what's happening this week? How is your golf game? Have you been to any new clubs?" Billy, in one minute, would catch up on an entire week's worth of action. "I heard the new girl in reservations is a real looker". Japes replied. "You know more than I do and you only are here one night a week. How do you do that? Everyone talks to me, I love being in the loop. The hotel keeps me connected."

Nobody knew what Billy did for a living, but everyone knew that he had plenty of money. Japes, after weeks of questioning, found out that Billy held a position as a buyer for a prestigious clothing store. He would fly to Empire City and Paris regularly to purchase various lines of women's clothes spending millions of dollars every year. "If you have 'the eye' and you buy the right designs at the right prices the store does well, it does very well. But, if you are unable to buy the right styles and colors you can destroy the business, " said Billy. "Wow! Why in the world do you work at a hotel? You certainly do not need the money,"said Japes. "The patrons my man the patrons that is why I am here. Life happens right in front of us every day; at the hotel, I see rich guests, poor guests, important guests, ugly guests, pretty guests, and any guest you can think of. I observe them when they are happy and I observe them when they are stressed, all the time, noting what they wear and what everyone says about each other. The hotel is a laboratory for me, and it helps me buy," declared Billy. " That is so cool, the hotel is working for you, not the other way around?" Queried Japes, "Isn't that great!" replied Billy.

All the servers Japes worked with were not as cool or sophisticated as Billy, and in fact countless simply worked for a paycheck. Not feeling pleasure from helping others, entrapped servers into a cumbersome psyche. Dan, from the "City of Cars" and Shirley, from the Badlands region both worked with Japes at the desk. Dan liked vodka and Shirley liked motorcycles. They were born into common working families who toiled and labored in factories for generations, therefore migrating to this area in hopes of starting a new life, seemed to be a fruitful idea, however, they remained entrenched in their ancestral mentality. "Why do you balance the house count, so quickly?" asked Dan. "So we know the available rooms and the rooms we can reserve." replied Japes. "That is too much work man, just keep checking them in and out, and let the manager take care of the details. After all, isn't that why they receive the enormous salaries?" asked Dan. "I like running the business and taking care of these guests, it is what we do." replied Japes. "No way we do not need to do that it's not our job! " Snorted Dan. Japes discovered the difference between happy servers and servers who merely existed while observing the actions of his befuddled coworkers. Shirley behaved the same as Dan although not quite as direct in her demeanor.

A country server with tattoos and a love for riding motorcycles, Shirley meticulously performed her duties, but never wanted to learn more than the task at hand. Perhaps this outlook started with her upbringing or maybe it was her own choice, but in the end, she and Dan were basic workers, and they were getting by with minimal effort and no responsibility. One day Dan arrived at work complaining he had caught a cold; he had the sniffles so he brought a container of orange juice, which he periodically took a drink of to soothe his scruffy, sore throat. Halfway through the shift Japes realized, Dan appeared pickled out of his mind, smelling of booze, the orange juice contained vodka, and unlike the chef back east that drank whiskey, Dan could not hold his liquor. Placing guests in occupied rooms, disconnecting telephone calls, and incorrectly posting charges to guest room accounts, expedited his demise. Japes covered as best he could, but Dan inevitably lost his job. Shirley would hang in until the end, but two weeks after Japes moved on she was forced to leave, unable to absorb the full responsibility of the desk.

Candy, the first server Japes had met from Horse Country, was a beautiful and elegant server, and in fact, had won her regions beauty pageant. Candy and Jennifer, the reservation manager, were close friends who always carried a smile and were fun to work with. They were easy on the eyes, an important prerequisite, which Mr. Suave enforced, requiring all front office servers to have "a great presentation", meaning all the girls were very attractive. One day Japes asked Candy "Would you and Jennifer like to attend a golf tournament? There is a great event up in the foothills this weekend and the legendary Sam Snead is playing. We can all make a day of it and have a picnic." "Well, sure Japes that sounds like summertime fun," replied Candy. Coming of age presents itself in many different ways, for Japes, spending the day with the pageant winner and the blonde bombshell encouraged his maturity. Maybe life involved more than work, as he could not believe these two charming girls wanted to hang with him. Not a day of courtship for the young server, but learning an important lesson, the girls confided in him while they watched the pro-golfers and soaked up the sun. "You are authentic Japes, we know you are honest and all you are looking for is to share your interest in golf with us. Most boys your age want to party, that makes you unusually refreshing." Mores from ones up-brining became the basis for interpersonal as well as organizational behavior.

That winter he befriended two foreign servers, Pat, a tall, skinny server who worked in room service, and his girlfriend Tricks who worked as a waitress. Inviting Pat and Trick to a professional basketball game, which neither had ever attended, or even seen since emigrating from Ireland, initiated the relationship. For some reason they never seemed to have any money, but were always upbeat and planning different activities. They had a great time at the game, but showed no interest in dining on a hot dog or even a box of popcorn in fact they did not eat or drink any food Japes became perplexed. "Why don't you two eat? You are undoubtedly hungry," said Japes. "We save our money for cocaine; we love our cocaine and snort it whenever we can. It is great for partying you can go at it all night long!" giggled Trick. Japes little brain went click, realizing they were hyper, skinny, and always doing something. It could not have been more obvious. "Would you like to do a bump Japes?" asked Trick. "No thanks, that's not how I roll", replied Japes. Encountering Pat and Trick during their search for the serious "drug crowd", highlighted the complexity of the hotel experience, and the practices within. This distraction, however, surfaced as a prevalent pastime within the hotel culture utilized by both patrons and servers alike.

The hotel in and of itself occupied most of Japes time. Mr. Greenback, a stockbroker from Empire City, always stayed at Japes hotel when visiting the area. He enjoyed Japes and counseled him every time he checked out that he should learn to be a stockbroker. Flattered by this interest from an accomplished executive, he finally told Mr. Greenback, "Thank you, but I am a hotelier it is in my blood. I chased the big paycheck once before and now I follow my instincts." Where else in the world could you experience people literally kissing you simply as a result of feeling welcome? Guests, oftentimes, take license to display themselves in fashions rarely seen in most walks of life, there are no two days that are the same when you work in a hotel, moreover the actions of guests intrigued Japes, and in fact he felt challenged to please them all. This proved to be a lofty ambition shared with the true hotel servers he came to know.

The Rooms, Executive, referred to as Olive Oil, was perfectly put together. The mistress of Mr. Suave, and the second in a long line of Kiva servers, commonly referred to as Brown Nose servers that Japes became involved with, played at managing. These Brown Nose servers did anything they could to keep their bosses happy, but rarely had a clue on doing their own job. Server's like Olive Oil were scattered within the hotel world, and although these ingratiating tactics were obvious, ironically if they applied these efforts towards what needed to be done they could have been successful. Inevitably, this selective behavior came back to bite them.

During a quiet weekend, Japes worked the desk by himself, with the switchboard operator named Millie. She resembled a muddleheaded server with a brain to match, whereby paying attention deemed not one of her strong suit' she spent the majority of her time painting her nails. Japes had informed Olive Oil that Millie presented a problem, but no remedy lay on the horizon. It appeared to be rather quiet that night so Japes occasionally wandered by the PBX area and asked Millie, "Any calls"? "No, nothing is going on." she replied. Two hours later Mr. Suave arrives screaming at Japes saying no one was answering the switchboard. Bewildered, they both walked over to the switchboard and discovered Millie decided to silence the ringer, while she concentrated on her grooming. Not good! Then, Olive Oil shows up and begins lecturing Japes on how to run a shift. She put on an impressive show for the old-man, despite knowing full well Millie should never have been there. Hoping the powers to be would see through these murky waters Japes remained silent.

Not long after, Japes experienced an event filled evening that would enhance his career. During the late night shift, a security guard asked Japes to take a walk with him. "What for?" asked Japes. "You will see replied the security guard". The two walked to the lobby and Gumshoes, the security guard, pointed up to a second floor balcony where, in full view of the entire lobby, in the only room with its lights on, two patrons were in the midst of a romantic encounter. The scene spotlighted quite the show for all to see. "Joe go knock on their door," said Japes. "I was on my way, but that was not the reason I came to get you. Follow me." said Joe. The two climbed up the stairs by the executive offices, and sprawled out halfway down the hall Japes noticed a server lying on the floor. What! Mr. Suave had passed out with a half empty glass of whiskey next to him, drunk and barely able to mumble his own name. Quickly, they helped Mr. Suave to his feet and escorted him to his office. A couch, positioned in the sitting area, acted as his bed for the evening. Nobody ever knew what happened, and Mr. Suave would never forget their' help.

During the next few months Japes proved himself to be a dedicated young manager while running the evening shift with a young server named Sid. Sid was not a Flathead, but he certainly acted like one. For no particular reason, the young server labeled Japes "Hawkeye "and he referred to himself as Pierce from the television show Mash. They displayed a positive, infectious attitude, which consequently made the job fun. Teasing each other and playing pranks with everyone and everything, while never forgetting about the guests, developed into the norm. This informal group power was attributed to the "fun and skill" they displayed. The interaction brought all the servers closer together as the group became a team. The focus directed on the banter between the two, and the environment they created grew into a common theme highlighting a key to success, therefore Japes did not dwell on their relationship, as he and Sid naturally put on a show. After a while, he realized that many servers did not enjoy the stage and all it had to offer. In fact, they did not participate in any meaningful activities whatsoever; it appeared as though life for too many proved just a chore, and subsequently they stopped learning and thinking on their own. The implied authority for those who did participate became real, and Japes knew Sid and his relationship and the fun they demonstrated created a recherche hotel environment. Every server gained from it and would continue long after they left, every server except Olive Oil, the quintessential Brown Nose.

One day the hotel, completely sold out, buzzed with excitement. In a large hotel normally that would not be a big deal, but that day at 4 PM there were fifteen arrivals and only two vacant rooms. To compound the situation, all of the arrivals were corporate customers who could care less about a free room at some other hotel. Most of these patrons were Bulls from varying industries, and they would not be fun to deal with. Rarely does a hotel walk a guest during the day as it usually occurs late at night after the hotel executives had gone home, that, however, would not be the case this day. Olive Oil and the entire staff were still at work when the fun started. A good leader would step up and professionally explain the situation to the guest and set the example. Japes effortlessly and without hesitation, walked every one of the guests, and felt obligated to do so. Berated and humiliated by some tough Bulls, while Olive Oil stood idly by, highlighted the reality of the Brown Nose upward leaper who did not care, and it never entered her mind to help, for she exhibited no executive skills, and would only exist as long as the boss controlled her. The vast majority of the staff, including "the brass", acted surprised at the day's events. In fact, a few servers spoke to Japes directly imploring him not to put up with the lack of support. It did not bother Japes since he empathized with the Bulls never taking it personally at the same time accepting the responsibility for the entire event.

Two weeks to the day Japes was asked to go to Mr. Suave's office. "Japes, I have been asked to offer you a position as an executive back in your neck of the woods. It is a smaller hotel, but has an excellent reputation within the community. I told my counterpart back in the Land of

69

Empires that you were loyal and easily took on responsibility." "Thank you. I truly appreciate the promotion," said Japes. It was wise to have never spoken to anyone about Mr. Suave's drinking indiscretion and Olive Oil's incompetence. Both his abilities as a manager and as a confidante distinguished him from the pack. He set his sights on the Land of Empires, and unlike his last few stops, he would be working in a resort environment. Stoked for his first real executive position, he started down the road to a small world away from the hustle and bustle of the major city. Again, although destined to leave his fellow servers who he had grown so close to, he knew it was the smart thing to do. The separation from yet another gang proved painful for the bond between servers remained strong, as every day for years they worked together to please others. The life developed into a true art, a true dedication, and a true love of being a server.

Executive

Japes traveled for almost three days before he arrived in the new world, a relaxing trip as the meandering trail passed many beautiful country estates a far cry from the bustling metropolis and quite unexpected. Arriving at the new hotel, nestled in the heart of this quaint elegant city, brought a surprising smile to the young hotelier. This would be the first time he worked at a Hilltop Hotel a chain known for its unparalleled commitment to customer service. Welcomed to the hotel by a nice young bellman he felt special, his new boss, however, away on vacation, allowed him to evaluate the lay of the land on his own. Although Japes served in hotels for a number of years he had never been an "executive". In fact, he was unsure as to what that even meant, but would soon find out.

Josie, the housekeeper manager, somehow found her way to his office on the first day. She offered Japes the first chance to tour the facility, and he felt encouraged to find a manager looking for him instead of the other way around. Josie, a wonderful server, belonged in the hotel business. She methodically worked her way up from being a maid, then a supervisor, and finally to overseeing the department. Growing up in the town carried distinct advantages for Josie, and Japes would discover the many labor challenges when recruiting maids in the Land of Empires. Being more concerned with taking care of the guests rather than providing for herself made her an exception to the rule. She would be difficult to replace under any set of circumstances. Josie would turn out to be the essence of a true server. Her daughter, Pawn, her assistant, worked as diligently as anyone, but allowed no time for Japes or anyone else for that matter.

During the tour, Josie introduced Japes to the engineer Steve. Working in the trenches for many years sculpted this heavyset, scruffy, indifferent about his appearance, man into a dead ringer of " Brutus" from the Popeye cartoons. Josie acted politely, but Japes could tell she barely tolerated his company. Steve did not bother to extend himself when greeting Japes simply saying hello, welcome to the hotel with a casual informal introduction. Josie continued to take Japes on the tour, as they went to the back of the house. The lobby and front entrance were quite beautiful and truly fit into the town, the back of the house, however, looked in terrible disrepair. The cafeteria, surrounded with dark grey concrete walls contained a small salad bar positioned to the side. Looking more like a prison cell, the eatery stood adjacent to the laundry and housekeeping departments, which were surrounded with the same concrete facade. The building, although it looked almost new on the outside, was in reality much older.

Japes entire focus changed from the hotel to the servers managing the hotel. He had been enamored with the excitement in the activities of the guests and the servers with whom he worked. Now, he became more curious about the managers he oversaw than the servers who interacted with the guests. A tremendous change in perspective, yet Japes still wanted to have fun the same as he enjoyed in his previous jobs, all the time knowing he needed to lead. His next introduction to Bobbin, the reservation manager, brought a smile to his face. She worked at the hotel for many years representing a happy server and possibly a bit of a racer at heart, she actively participated in hotel activities, and became a true friend to Japes. Bobbin lived in the town her entire life and knew everybody in the community. This relationship gave him great insight not only into the hotel world, but also into the community. The last server who he met that day was the front office manager Nod. Describing Nod would be difficult, as at first sight, he appeared to be a worker displaying a muscular physique who carried himself professionally with a calm demeanor. He too lived his entire life in the town. Japes noticed while making the tour and visiting with Nod that he drove an expensive car. Unlikely that a manager in his position could afford such a car, peaked Japes curiosity, thus beginning his pilgrimage to executive status.

The hotel manager showed up one week after Japes had started his new job. OC was not a Bull; he would be categorized more as one who uses the art of persuasion. Hailing from the Midland Region of the country, he brought wonderful family values and a sense of partnership to the Land of Empires. Not a traditional manager, he walked a fine line between taking care of his home and taking care of his business. You would not categorize him as being slick, but you would say he acted quite clever and knew not to push too hard. He appeared grateful that Japes had been transferred in as a new player, since the majority of the management staff grew up in the area, and there were only a few managers who possessed backgrounds in other hotels. This immediate recognition bonded OC to Japes resulting in implied power for the new guy as a result of his background. OC's evaluation of the hotel and the staff differed from what Japes observed when touring with Josie. OC managed the hotel as he wished while Japes both learned from him and carried out his requests. OC's secretary, Sniffy, a petite server, wore virtually nothing, and apparently would partake in the same drugs that the wacky couple had enjoyed back in Mountain City. Her qualifications for this job, therefore, simply entailed showing up, furnishing the boss someone with whom he could flirt. Not a coherent plan, if he pursued an executive position in a major business, however, the arrangement worked just fine out in the country.

The food and beverage manager who relocated from the Midland Region with OC was named Willie. Willie epitomized a Bull, a real husky Bull with a solid background. Eating and drinking consumed most of his free time, as this enormous server embodied the culinary as well as libation culture. He appeared defensive when discussing his areas of responsibility and did not like anyone challenging his restaurant's performance or the quality of his food. Japes had years of experience in this area, but remained careful not to criticize Willie's restaurants. After all, it was not the Ritz and there was no need to be perfect all the time. Willie, a wonderful server, portrayed a typical Bull persona on the outside, but when one pulled back all the bravado a true straight shooter glared you in the eye. Willie looked like a German with a square jaw, a firm handshake, and a measured response to any engagement. He recognized that he ate and drank too much and that he easily became defensive. In many respects he stood above the rest as he recognized the need to improve. Servers seldom admit they have to make changes to their lives. His assistant, Janet, with whom he confided on all matters concerning both the restaurant and the banquet operations, purported to be his ally and unfortunately drank just as much as Willie. She, however, did not embrace the beverage consumption issue and never felt the need for change. Failing to encourage the big guy where he truly needed help, cast her into the realm of an enabler.

Next in the parade of managers OC introduced him to Kick the controller. The controller at the hotel took care of all the financial business. It represented an important position as he met with the owners to discuss the monthly P&L statement, cash flow report etc. Encompassing the antithesis of a true server, this "local executive" based his entire career on financial analysis and his experience within that hotel. One would say he acted like a big server in a small world. He did not, however, have experience outside that community. Servers like Kick believed money and profits should always dictate how a hotel operated. Kick, completely void of fun, felt he could operate the hotel better than the general manager. Beliefs like this were typical, as most did not realize that the hotel business evolved around working with and taking care of staff with the exact same commitment and zeal one would give a patron. The better you performed these two disciplines the better the profits would be. The only true business decision for the hotels occurred long before executives, managers and workers showed up. The true business decision involved the location of the facility and the cost to build.

Handy, the Director of Sales, and the last of the "executives" that Japes would initially meet, personified a Racer who had recently relocated all the way from "Bikini

City". He loved the nose-candy, which went hand-in-hand with his hyperactive behavior. Servers typically have a good attention span, but Handy possessed the attention span of a gnat. OC and Handy were close, as OC knew that outside sales dictated the key to the success of this hotel. Handy performed magnificently, at his job, but he had many difficulties living in the small community. In fact, his apartment appeared in such disarray, that one would think a hobo lived there. He constantly dined out, he rarely stopped partying, and he never even dreamed of organizing his pad. A joy to be around Handy kept anyone who would listen in stitches. Interacting on another level with the customers and carrying on mesmerizing conversations did not, however, ingratiate him to the local servers who worked at the hotel. He knew this job would simply be a stepping-stone for him and his career. His fiancée, Mercedes, a beautiful girl who came to visit every month, soon appeared obvious in her aspirations to never settle down in this small town. Expectations for her and Handy were very high, and did not involve the quaint, country lifestyle. Japes, however, would remain friends with them for many years.

One of the traditions, which OC kept alive, included a mandatory cocktail at five PM every day. OC, Japes, Willie, and Handy would meet in the cocktail lounge on the top floor of the hotel for two martinis every Monday through Friday. Japes, a fair drinker, could not believe this happened every single day. This eclectic group of servers who all came from different backgrounds with a wide range of experiences, bellied up to the bar religiously. OC developed influence over everyone, and would apply this style to manage these new executives. Servers like to be comfortable and appreciated the same amenities the guests for whom they would serve. If nothing else, the four held one common activity. They all enjoyed two cocktails every night at five PM.

When Japes immersed himself into the management of the front office, he realized the small staff possessed little experience with hospitality and the nuances necessary to take care of customers. He previously worked in large cities with demanding customers. Now, he faced the reality of dealing with demanding customers and unskilled servers. One server in particular, Sneaky, did not acquire the skills necessary to work in the front office. Nod previously hired him to this position as a favor to his nephew. Japes, determined to develop a great group of servers who catered to all the customers needs, learned the hard way that this would be a difficult task. After many counseling sessions, Japes decided to let Sneaky go, despite not being familiar with unemployment and the responsibilities of an executive. After time passed, Japes was summoned to a hearing to explain the circumstances surrounding Sneaky's termination. Japes explained, to the best of his ability, that Sneaky lacked the qualifications required to perform his duties. The judge, however, felt differently, and insisted Sneaky could have stayed in his position. Like many outsiders, dramatically unaware as to what it took to service customers in a hotel, he simply looked at attendance and basic requirements of the position. Japes, although severely reprimanded by the judge, was not required to rehire Sneaky, and realizing Sneaky could perform fine in a different job agreed to be more careful. Japes, however, never again terminated a server simply because they were not right for the job, and he worked diligently to hire the right server for the right position. Realizing he barely interacted with any of the customers at the hotel, the shine had faded from the apple. After the first few months as an executive he dedicated his time focusing on the staff. He wondered, other than having a drink together, could these executives secure some fun?

Hoteliers for the most part are fun-loving creatures, enjoying the simple pleasures of life and not burdening themselves with the impressions of others. That is to say, live and let live so long as you do not hurt another. The hotel world provided a bastion of this life for Japes to thrive. Now, faced with a real world situation, was he to improve his life and compromise his values or could he still cultivate fun and move forward. Observations revealed that most Bulls and leaders, he encountered, demonstrated no sense of humor and remained serious, as they did not display or open up to any conversation pertaining to their personal lives, families, and in particular emotions. In the most basic sense, this represented an original form of discrimination. A strange phenomenon, as the essence of a hotel centered around taking care of all those needs for customers and staff alike. Must an executive mask all these interactions or could they simply be honest? Japes decided to take the honest route, and in his career he met only one other hotel executive who did the same. This determination would turn out to be the correct path.

The Empire group needed to have some fun, and although Japes was not the top dog he took it upon himself to bring servers together. Drinking emerged as the one common theme amongst the group, he, therefore, recruited Bob, his car insurance man, a local, lifelong resident who grew up in the area and knew everybody and every pub within ten miles, to navigate the terrain. Exclaiming "gin drinks", with a tremendous grin every time he saw Japes, qualified Bob to become the tour-guide to some of the finest local establishments. Willie, in particular, gained expertise on all the local beers and wines distilled in the region. The area provided a plethora of fantastic five-star restaurants, and OC decided the hotel would pay for some extravagant meals at these restaurants. Happy these gatherings involved little talk concerning work and focused on life and families reassured Japes instincts. He knew this initiated a good beginning for the young executives, and although OC never truly open up to the group he made strides in that direction. Forever remaining one who influenced, in his own way, he accorded Japes an invaluable lesson showing him an avenue to bring perspective and teamwork to the forefront.

Another activity, Japes brought to the table, included golf. Although some of the servers were not golfers they agreed to participate in occasional outings. Playing golf since he was just a youngster, he loved the game and everything the game brought to him. An average competitor, but more importantly, he felt equal in all respects to the people he played with, an important as well as dynamic consideration for one with a disability. A game requiring integrity, sportsmanship, competition, and honesty exposed ones character. There were many courses in the Land of Empires and the group played all of them. Willie traveled along so he could partake in the 19th hole at the various clubhouses'. Winning or losing meant nothing during these outings, it cultivated laughter and personal friendship. The one benefit tournament the group played in took place at an exclusive private country club, and the hoteliers stood out like a sore thumb amongst the aristocrats. They did not win the tournament, but they savored a great time. Japes, particularly taken back, observed the head aristocrat, thirty years his senior, giving his date a French- kiss hello at the celebratory banquet. This musty old fool thought he owned the world, but the night turned out just fine, as soon thereafter, his wife screaming in his ear, hurriedly escorted him out the door.

Japes became a better executive with the realization that the hotel family expanded. He spent his time working with his managers and executives, and his philosophy to keep everyone motivated and happy with their' lives and responsibilities evolved. Although he always felt working directly with the customer proved his favorite and most rewarding job, he knew he would never survive without expanding his horizons. Oftentimes, he jumped out to the front desk participating in what he loved, and wanting everyone to feel the same when serving others. So the first true decision, which came across his desk concerning Nod, marked a big one. A local, who always showed up to work, dressed immaculately, and by all accounts interacted well with the staff members, appeared peculiar displaying the traits of a Red-eyed server. Japes had seen this before, but it had always represented a server who liked to drink. Nod did not like to drink, but he liked his drugs. In fact, he supplied the drugs throughout the hotel and more importantly throughout the community. What should Japes do? He could not be direct with Nod because he had no real facts. The judge would have had a field day with him. He could not bring it to the executive level, as it would be put back on him to move Nod out. In essence, Nod fulfilled his job duties despite always being blurry eye'd. Japes decided to do nothing. He would let the events speak for themselves and let the community dictate the decision.

The excitement of the daily interaction with people from all different walks of life was replaced with the daily interactions of the staff and executives. A different world within the world he had known in the beginning, and it seemed quite odd, that the servers who were rewarded the most financially were the ones who in reality provided the least amount of service to the guests. One would think the servers who took care of customers would be those who deserve the greatest rewards. Indeed the servers with the great skills were few and far between. Japes learned that this hierarchy related directly to the amount of responsibility not to one's skill level. Engaging with, and providing for a patron is the backbone of any successful hotel. It seemed to him the key to a successful business required blending these two philosophies. There could be no barrier between the executives and the workers everyone had to be equal when it came to servicing the guests. The more types of influence the young hotelier exerted the greater his power. The power to motivate and create a thriving culture.

During a 4th of July celebration Handy and Mercedes announced they would be leaving this small world in The Land of Empires. OC became stressed beyond belief, as his friend was on his way back to "Bikini City". He tried to persuade Handy to stay but to no avail. The relocation inevitable, as Mercedes skill in persuasion far outweighed the alternative. Japes too would miss Handy, as they had become close friends and drinking partners.

The company sent a number of candidates from all over the country to replace Handy. OC, although he would make the final decision, let Willie and Japes meet with the prospective candidates. A jovial sales manager from High-falls, named Sot, appeared particularly animated. He stood out as an endearing and persuasive Red-eyed server. The second one Japes encountered in less than six months. He could sell anything. His family, heavily involved with car sales back in the High-falls area, groomed him for his future. A handsome young man who always had a smile on his face, and mischief in his eyes, he told stories of selling cars to people and using unscrupulous tactics to get the sale. One story involved the sale of a car to a lady who was not certain she could afford it. Knowing, if he could get her to drive the car for the weekend, that she would love it, and feeling confident the sale would come to fruition, he plotted his scheme. As she began to decline the offer to take the car for the weekend, Sot dropped her car keys down a drain in the parking lot. Unable to retrieve her keys she reluctantly took the new car, when she returned on the following Monday the deal was done, he would do anything to close a sale.

Sot, hired by OC despite all his faults, sold the hotel with the finesse of a seasoned veteran. For a server who grew up selling cars for a living to move up to an executive position and sell hotel rooms represented pure joy. He had no trouble fitting in at the five o'clock cocktail hour. He and Willie had their differences as Sot could easily get under a servers skin. He exhibited no service skills, strictly a sales server, and his actions would magnify the significant difference between the two. The agreement consummated early on that Sot would sell the rooms and leave everything else to the operations staff. Unfortunately, he also became close friends with Nod. You can imagine when two Red-eye servers get together what the consequences might be. One winter, Sot sold a series of ski tours to stay at the hotel. He would offer a late-night dance party with drinks and hors d'oeuvres to seal the deal. Sot, of course, would personally greet and stay until the wee hours of the night to hold the hand of the event coordinator. He and Nod along with the ski tour director were high as kites every weekend. The ski tour guests used every towel, bar of soap, and amenity they could get their hands on. It involved a tremendous amount of work for virtually no profit. These Red-eyed servers were starting to affect the business, but the faithful guests would soon let the hotel know what should be done. Eventually, the ski tours were canceled as many regular guests were disturbed and would not come back to the hotel. The last thing you want to do in a hotel is lose your loyal patrons to another. Nod's drug sales took a financial hit as the tour business was cancelled.

One phenomenon, unique to this world in the Land of Empires, included an event called camp weekend, where for two days every year, in the middle of the summer, all of the parents would come from the Empire City to visit their children. Youngsters from wealthy families stayed in various camps throughout the area for eight weeks, religiously, every year. These camps were quite exclusive and varied from all boys to all girls to coeds with many different age groups. For some of the young campers it served as an extension of their school, and indeed, many of the parents only saw their children for a few weeks every year. Needless to say, the area commanded a great demand for hotel rooms when all of these parents came to visit their children. Japes had already worked in major cities and met many famous and powerful leaders. When everyone told him about this particular event he thought nothing of it. He did not know what he was getting into. If the hotel had overbooked by even one room there were no other accommodations available for over one hundred miles. Families would rent spare bedrooms in their homes as a result of this great demand. The weekend traffic, compounded by the renowned performances given at Spangleweed, invaded the quaint village. This outdoor amphitheater hosted great orchestras every weekend throughout the summer.

Nod supervised his usual shift on the Friday night of camp weekend. Amazed at all of the cars steadily pulling up to the entry, Japes recognized Bentleys, Ferraris, Jaguars, and even a few Mercedes for the not so wealthy. There is wealth and then there is real wealth. This represented real wealth and indeed some of these patrons could have bought the hotel outright. Nod, unfortunately at one in the morning stood sold out with no available rooms. Mr. Wolf a true Bull from the Empire City had reserved and pre-paid for two guest rooms. Japes received a call from Nod at one in the morning asking him what he should do. Japes knew they were not overbooked when he left and wondered how Nod created such a situation, nonetheless, this would not solve the issue at hand. Under Japes direction, using all his connections and local knowledge to find Mr. Wolf some accommodations, Nod survived the onslaught. It would have taken Japes a long time to drive to the hotel and at that point there was nothing he could do. The next day, when meeting with Nod and Bobbin, he profusely apologized for putting them in such a situation. The truth came out, Nod had given rooms' to a customer who did not have a reservation, and this powerful, wealthy man finagled his way into the hotel claiming they had lost it. For the rest of his tenure at that hotel Japes realized he would engage directly with these customers. The entire incident featured such bizarre behavior, whereby these rich condescending bully's expected this country hotel to perform like the Plaza or the Pierre. Japes addressed the staff for the only time that summer stating, "One can put a crown on a server and dress them up, but they will always be a server not a prince. You all are wonderful servers keep it up!" This delineated his interpretation of the circumstances, and without berating the affluent customers insane expectations he complimented the entire staff.

The head of security at the hotel, Dickey, spent his entire life in the community, serving the bulk of his career as a police detective with intimate knowledge of all the town officials. A happy gentleman who Japes immediately bonded with, Dickey appeared to be a Red-Faced server, a typical attribute of this healthy breed of server. His only vice involved gambling and taking many trips to the Casinos' with his cronies. Providing Japes important information concerning all the activities in the hotel, as well as being a great jokester who kept everybody laughing, necessitated his role. Observing key personnel, who normally would not be supervised, including Elm, the very eligible hotel's piano player, occupied his evenings. Elm, constantly pursued by the local girls, kept Dickey on his toes and within clear sight at all times. The girls flocked to watch him play in the lounge. Adjacent to the lounge, a pool area surrounded by hotel guest rooms and a large outdoor- deck, acted as ground zero. The floor of the pool would be raised to the level of the main floor and the surrounding lobby. This area then would become a dance floor over the water, a unique way of utilizing space and attracting many from the neighboring communities. During his break Dickey would often catch Elm in a guest room with an enamored fan tickling something other than the ivories.

Sot and Willie would butt heads all the time. It kept everyone involved and as one manager used to say, "If we were all the same the world would be a boring place, in fact, isn't that what makes the world go round?" Sot earned a terrible reputation for drinking too much. On one occasion he hosted a Super Bowl party at his home, at halftime, he realized he had drunken all the beer and wine, which had been purchased for the party. He summoned the audacity to raid the hotel and take liquor from the hotel liquor room to return home for his own consumption. One might say Sot did have a problem. He explained to OC the following Monday that the liquor-store was closed so he simply borrowed liquor from the hotel. OC made it perfectly clear that it would be the last time Sot ever touched the liquor room key. During this debacle Willie became livid, as he of course held the responsibility for all the liquor in the hotel. One argument led to another and the two decided to make a bet. They bet one hundred dollars that neither one of them could stop drinking for one month. The first to give in would be required to pay the other one hundred dollars. Willie was an honorable server, but many associates were deputized to keep an eye on Sot.

After a couple of weeks it was rumored that Willie had resumed drinking beer. Sot had been the one everyone, including his wife Patty, kept an eye on. When Sot got wind of the situation he became determined to find out the truth, so he recruited another server to spy on Willie. Willie, an enormous Bull, who spent the majority of his free time alone in his apartment, located on the third floor of a building adjacent to the traffic circle in the middle of town, sat perusing the television channels. That night Sot and his cohort snuck out with a ladder and climbed a tree so they could spy into Willie's living room. Willie sat in his briefs, drinking beer after beer, while Sot, horrified at the vision, but elated with the drinking, quickly erupted when his cohort pointed out that the beer was root beer. Sot became so distraught he immediately scurried to the local pub and started to drink. He did not know which horrified him more, seeing Willie in his skivvies or losing the one hundred dollar bet.

This was not the first time Japes had made a friend, but this time it felt different. Although he and Sot were different both in their upbringing and their attitudes they each appreciated the differences. Sot learned about "The Hotel Business" from Japes and shared an interest in sports, gambling, and general fun together. Japes learned about a "young family" as Sot married a great wife and became a father to a beautiful daughter. Japes had not eaten a home cooked meal for years until the two hit it off. Hoteliers spend the majority of their time inside the hotel working within a close-knit group. This evolved into the first "outside" relationship with any real substance. Although Sot did not appear to be a true server, he personified the quintessential salesman. He simply required sound, and thoughtful guidance with "the big picture".

And so this illustrated the life of a server in this Land of Empires. One day OC approached Japes and asked if he was interested in a promotion. Japes said of course, what would that entail. "You would have to fly to "Gray City" and interview for a Room Executive position in a five hundred room hotel," stated OC. Excited to further his career, he made the journey to a dark and gloomy city where the hotel connected to an airport. Japes entered the hotel and immediately greeted by a tiny Bull named Mohammed. Mohammed, the general manager, escorted him on a tour of the facility and then invited him dinner. The hotel, badly worn down, and Mohammad, acting more like a dictator than a manager, left a scary impression. Nothing about this experience impressed Japes aside from the large increase in salary. The next day, he thanked Mohammed for his hospitality and told him his decision would be forthcoming. Upon returning to the resort hotel he informed OC and others

91

that this would not work for him. Quality of life was more important than money. His instincts would serve him well in the future.

THE CHANGE

OC managed the hotel for almost two years, and as a family man, he did everything to take care of his wife and children, despite their longing for the life back in the Midlands. Finally, after much consideration, OC decided to leave the company. Leaving the organization that promoted him to general manager occurred not because he felt ungrateful, not because he did not make a fair salary, but simply to return home to his family and friends. Japes, accustomed to change in the hotel business, traversed the walking plank between coming and going many times. This point of demarcation, however, unearthed the raw emotions of feeling uncertain about the future. To compound the situation Willie agreed to relocate with OC. They were buddies long before the move to the Land of Empires and he too wanted to go home. Leaving a tremendous void at the five o'clock hour for those who had become so close, Japes would miss the home-cooked meals at OC's house, the golf outings, the cocktails, and the combative nature between Willie and Sot. Change can be beneficial, but it is not necessarily easy, for the increased degree of interdependence between these executives created a relationship far beyond that of minimal tasks.

Only a short period of time passed before the new manager arrived. He hailed from the Mountain City, where

Japes had worked, and they both knew a lot of the same servers. This comforted Japes, as it always felt nice to have common acquaintances. Van, the new manager, an enduring Racer, a seasoned veteran with a strong food and beverage background, had never been a general manager. He had a lot to prove to himself and to his superiors. A Racer, still holding worker tendencies, Van stayed in terrific physical condition and maintained the energy to keep up with anyone. He oftentimes worked seven days in a row without taking time off, showing his dedication to the business and proving in the long run to be a good hotelier.

With this change came a period of enlightenment for Japes. Open-minded to whatever the new manager wanted, but smart enough to realize why the servers moved so much. It equated to moving from one family to another. Ending the golf and the cocktail hour while focusing entirely on the work placed Van in a provocative category. He measured managers and executives by the amount of hours they spent at the hotel. Real "old-school" dictated one to be at the hotel at least six days a week, and it did not matter how well the hotel performed or how poorly the hotel performed the executives simply needed to be there. There were times when Van literally slept under his desk' as he slipped from his chair in exhaustion. Japes remained dedicated but he thought this to be ridiculous. In the beginning, Sot captured any opportunity he could to cause mischief, crap all over Van,

and make fun of his style. Van knew nothing about sale
Sot easily played him like a fiddle. It would take time to see
what would happen to this world as Van quickly settled in.

One night, in the middle of the summer, Japes woke
out of a sound sleep with a startling revelation about a girl he
knew when growing up in Vacationland. She embodied the
meaning of service through and through despite the fact that
she did not work in a hotel. Her demeanor and giving nature
were a true giveaway. Japes, not a believer in fantasy, or
carrying any strong religious values, experienced a vision
that night which he never forgot. His classmate, Janeen, who
he knew in high school and had become good friends with,
gently waved goodbye to him in his sleep. He had not seen
or spoken to Janeen for several years since their lives had
taken them in separate directions. Married and starting a
new life she and her husband had relocated halfway across
the country to live in the Mountain Region. Japes became so
startled by the vision that he called his mother that same
morning asking her about Janeen and her family. His mom
hesitated, and then she told him Janeen recently had died
from a terrible disease, that it was a shock to the community
and to everybody who knew and loved her. Japes did not
know what to say and he did not know what to think. This
involved something that could never be explained and would
stay in his mind the rest of his life. She appeared as clear as
a bell flying away, waving her hand at him, all the while he

felt both frightened and heartbroken. Remembering an entire dream for the only time in his young life, further instilled in him the belief that all servers were connected and true spirits would stay together forever.

Feeling inspired and in a real sense awakened to life, Japes decided to venture out on his own and interview at hotels near Cod City. He received an informational interview at a hotel that looked like a castle. He did his research and found that the company was growing, and that they would need knowledgeable executives. Although he was not offered a job, he could wait, as the group appeared to be building for the future. Moving around the country dispirited Japes, so he looked at organizations that were limited to a small area.

For the annual employee party Van decided the executives would serve dinner to all line staff. Japes visibly displayed great difficulty in lifting trays of food to carry to the tables as a result of his dystrophy. He remained as close to the line staff as any executive had ever been and as a result he enjoyed honest friendships'. The idea that he should carry something, which appeared extremely difficult for him, they found offensive. Japes, being compliant to the new manager, and wanting to please, with a lot of help from some servers, managed to get through the service. He thought to himself this manager cannot see beyond the nose on his face. Everyone is not a worker we all have a role to play.

Japes, soon thereafter, received an offer with the opportunity to move to Cod City and manage at the hotel that looked like a castle. The only knowledge he gathered concerning the new group was that they were in one geographical area. Accepting Japes resignation and two weeks notice emboldened Van, who decided to give him a hard time, instructing him to go into forty guest rooms, each afternoon to clear the dirty sheets and unload the laundry carts. Van thought it important to engage in physical work to help the shortfall in staffing for Josie. Japes again complied with his wishes, although he physically exhibited an awkward distress. Josie, embarrassed for Japes, as he supported her in many ways over the years, came to his rescue, ultimately proving to himself that he chose the right path. He had reached far beyond his physical limitations, but like many with his challenges, the desire to "fit in" far outweighed common sense. Respecting Van as a result of his position at the hotel, but not for his actions strengthened his resolve. "We are what we do" did not mean what we physically did. Van had a lot to learn. Japes left his friend Sot, and although this change had occurred many times before he somehow knew they would stay connected. A strange bond he and Sot shared, in fact, he demonstrated many poor characteristics that most would find obnoxious. Only time would tell what would evolve.

97

THE CASTLE

Japes had worked in larger hotels out in the mountain region, however, this hotel would turn out to be the most challenging of his career for many different reasons. Enjoying an early spring baseball game at fabulous Fenway highlighted a tremendous welcome to town, where he watched some big character named Clemons strike out twenty batters. It felt so cold that day Japes figured the pitcher simply wanted to get into the warmth of the clubhouse. Located not far from "Cod City" at the crossroads of two major highways, and immediately adjacent to a shopping plaza, enabled the sprawling, ornate hotel to attract many. The outside of the hotel looked like a castle, with towers in various locations all connected by hallways while the grounds sparkled with perfectly manicured beds of flowers and various perennial plantings. The doormen and bellmen wore beefeater outfits, which spotlighted quite an impression. The lobby itself, nothing spectacular and indeed appearing small for such a large hotel, appeared incredibly busy. The hotel located at the crossroads of the two major highways resulted in weekend traffic nightmares. Dozens of travelers, at the last minute, oftentimes decided to spend the night until the traffic cleared the next day. As a result, the front office would handle as many as one hundred unexpected walk-ins. This presented a real challenge with scheduling in order to accommodate these sudden arrivals.

The company portfolio consisted of four castle hotels scattered around the city; these hotels were built by and owned by Mr. Harsh. A self-made billionaire who built an empire of real estate, including hundreds of apartment buildings all around the city, and developing millions of square feet of commercial space used by many proved no small feat. His latest venture included the development of the hotels, which he loved so much. Mr. Harsh, a relentless workaholic, expected everyone who worked for him to work hard and to work every day. His reputation as a businessman equated to that of a cutthroat developer, and he stepped on less resourceful people to build his empire, unfortunately he held no concept or understanding of how to manage a hotel. Yet, he built and developed a number of enormous properties, and by pure luck two of the four were in perfect locations and proved to be quite successful. Frequently, he traveled at all hours of the day randomly visiting these properties, walking through and pointing out various shortfalls such as tape on the carpet or torn vinyl in a hallway, a bizarre, obsessive behavior for one so successful.

Japes new boss, Shorty, a young Bull with a great sense of humor ruled the roost. Full of youthful energy he managed a challenging property. The organization's evolution appeared so new and limited in its resources, that the overabundance of executive problems became painfully evident. Japes, in fact, appointed as the first Room Executive the company ever hired, created his own routine. Shorty and his assistant were the two executives who oversaw this three hundred and seventy five room property. Each of the department managers directed a large number of assistants and supervisors to carry out the daily activities. Shorty and his assistant were required to supervise over thirty managers in an extremely busy hotel an insane assignment to think it could work effectively. Shorty performed exceptionally considering how many servers he oversaw on a daily basis. Impossible with this set up to develop any real rapport and to build a team, Shorty prevailed. Business and politics were at the forefront, as there was no time for team building and basic management. After settling in, Japes learned that he would be required to work six days a week. Informed of this after he moved from his prior hotel and into the new world, felt deceptive. Not only was it required of him to work six days, he oversaw the hotel from 8 AM until 6 PM every Sunday.

The front office, poorly run, employed servers who worked and greeted the customers in an unfriendly manner, were not smiling, and did not seem concerned about the travelers. Ron, the front office manager, a gay server, hired all his close friends to work at the desk. Working diplomatically to convince Ron that this idea invited controversy, and carefully pointing out that diversity was not the issue, but hiring servers who enjoyed helping others would cultivate success fell on deaf ears. Ron could care less what Japes believed, as he had no intention of staying for long. All-in the revenue manager was not gay, a natural server with an endless amount of energy. He and Japes got along famously and became more than just work associates. All-in, an excellent revenue manager, motivated to move up the ladder to be an executive, showed promise. Shorty told Japes that as long as he managed the hotel All-in would not become the front office manager. He asked Shorty, why? "Last year a customer screamed at the desk and made threatening gestures towards All-in. All-in lost his cool and jumped over the desk, physically threatening to hurt the patron. I didn't care about the explanation I just stuck him in the back," stated Shorty. "Oh, I can see your point that doesn't seem very hospitable now does it," said Japes. The two never spoke about this again, but Japes believed all servers and especially All-in deserved a second chance. He revealed himself to be a true server with an exceptional level of energy, a handsome young man, who reminded one of another "Cod City Fellow" Jay Leno. Popular with the entire staff, he was known to be a "go to" guy.

On both the line staff and management alike, the hotel generated emotional stress. It caused tension, primarily resulting from the sheer volume of business with thousands of guests checking in and out every year. Second, the intensity magnified as a result of the owner demanding everyone to work such long hours. Third, the hotel's union invited confusion and ambiguity with a confrontational relationship between management and associates. Last, the hotel literally built by the owner himself, demanded all structures remain immaculate. That is to say, the owner employed his own construction group which built the hotel and expected every physical aspect to be like new, another ridiculous expectation.

Mac, the hotel engineer, born a proud Scottish server, raised in the Overland territory with a strong work ethic ruled over the physical structure. He helped build one of the additions to the original hotel many years earlier, developing relationships with all of the construction players who toiled in the different divisions. Mac oversaw a large department, which operated as one of the few departments not in the union. He employed a full-time carpenter, plumber, and many mechanics. He carried a lot of weight with Mr. Harsh as a result of doing a phenomenal job keeping the monstrous property in good shape. Mac also dated the executive secretary Hot-hips, so he covered all the bases, while maintaining open communications with the corporate staff. Mac kept in good shape and implemented a strict work regiment. Years of laboring at the shipyard enabled him to be well versed in all the trades. His practical knowledge anchored the cornerstone of his career, and indeed shaped his personal interests. His favorite hobby, boating, found him many a day cruising the local harbors of the Atlantic. Whether it be for an afternoon of striper fishing or sightseeing, he loved the life. It became a home away from home with all the creature comforts.

Sergey, the executive housekeeper managed the most difficult department Japes could possibly have imagined. A line server who Shorty promoted to a management position, she managed a number of assistants and supervisors who loved her and would help her do anything. She was not, however, a manager. The union flexed its muscle the most in this department, which made it virtually impossible to get the line staff to do their jobs. The union regulations dictated that the maids did not have to reach over their heads to dust. This motion considered too difficult and a risk to their health, and as a result the housemen were put on a schedule periodically going through every guest room to complete the dusting. They also went to every guest room and cleaned the upper portions of the bathroom walls. The hotel, never cleaned properly, somehow always maintained its four star rating, an early indication of Shorty's political prowess with the franchise. Sergey toiled half of her days in meetings with the union reps over ridiculous grievances. As bad as this was the laundry was even worse. This department ran twenty-four hours a day, seven days a week. The overnight servers were all young high school dropouts. To handle the demands of the hotel, the laundry and the limited equipment, which the servers had to work with, fell short of the mark. The laundry chute, which ran up seven floors and emptied into a room twenty feet long and ten feet wide, constantly filled with soiled bedding. This room was never empty of dirty linen. In fact, the only solution to keep up with the demand involved opening new linens and towels on a regular basis so that the guest could eat in the restaurant and stay in the guest rooms. This was a disaster, which could have been solved with new equipment, but despite many recommendations it would be ignored.

Killer, the banquet manager, could be the poster boy of a Racer. Receiving his nickname as a consequence of his narrow build and rapid pace motivated him to supervise a number of assistants who faithfully helped him set up and service the hundreds of events carried out every year. His close associate was Betty, the restaurant manager. Betty, like Sergey, started as a worker who Shorty promoted into management. She enjoyed a lot of leeway, as Shorty did not want to be involved and spend his time at the restaurant. The restaurant made no money and was strictly an amenity to the facility. On the other hand, the banquet department made a lot of money and required a lot of oversight.

Elko and Speedo were the receivers; they were both workers' but earned a little more authority than the average bear. Elko took care of the paperwork and Speedo did all the heavy lifting. They carried responsibility for the inventories, including the liquor room, and were required to stock the portable bars for banquets. The hotel purchased so many items that bidding out various vendors for the best prices proved vital for cost control. An expert at this, Elko, finagled savings, which even impressed Mr. Harsh. All the girls loved Speedo he looked as handsome as he was strong. The two made a good team and represented the hotel well.

Classee, the Director of Sales and Marketing, portrayed a stylish peddler of influence. Growing up in the city and developing a working knowledge of all the various markets put her in a powerful position. Holding her first position as a sales director, she proved to be a success. Well respected by both the sales and operational staff, oftentimes she jumped in to help the staff while setting up an event. She exuded cool and her style reminded one of a stylish smooth seller. Occasionally, she was found hanging in her office smoking a little rope. Frankly, one could not tell if she had been smoking all day or not at all as she always acted the same. Classee and Japes became friends for life and reconnected many times in the future.

Mellow, the executive chef ascended the ranks in the same fashion as a number of servers, promoted by Shorty from a line position, illustrating a worker who tried hard, but was unable to manage. Japes spent years in kitchens and worked with executive chefs as well as line cooks. Mellow was no chef. For all of Shorty's humor and energy he authored poor decisions by promoting servers who did not possess the skills necessary to qualify for the jobs. Constantly managing day-to-day situations that should have been handled by properly placed managers, all the while keeping the ship afloat solely with his energy level, screamed inexperience.   Amazed that this man, only one year his senior, managed the hotel, it seemed apparent to Japes that his organizational skills were required for the future of the company. This, however, would not turn out to be the reason why.

Maggie, the head of the health club, was a Bull, who carried more responsibility on a daily basis than many of the other managers. Shorty gave her carte blanche and let her do her own thing all the time. The health club, larger in comparison to most clubs located within a hotel, appeared quite unusual to Japes, as this department was usually an amenity for the guests to use. The Castle, however, attracted such a large, local health club participation that they collected on five hundred annual memberships. Including a racquetball court, a full set of Nautilus equipment, a steam room, a sauna room, and an Olympic size pool the club appealed to many. During the summer months an outside pool and a cabana for relaxing were utilized. After a period of time, Japes realized why this area garnered such attention.

Mrs. Harsh utilized the club three times a week, and Mr. Harsh frequented the health club every day. They liked Maggie and she could do no wrong. No wonder Shorty gave her free reign she lived a charmed, life demonstrating the perfect example of the golden rule, "He who has the gold rules".

Jitters', the assistant general manager, typified a skittish server, and in Japes career he had never observed a server so under qualified be placed in a position of authority. Jitters had a little bit of a Kiva in him as he always did what Shorty told him to do. Independent thinking and decision making, appeared painfully difficult for Jitters, as he constantly appeared nervous whether conducting a meeting or simply walking the hall. An honest server and a good citizen of the hotel but placed in the wrong role for someone so ill-prepared. He was seen from time to time in the public space of the hotel conversing with Mr. London. Mr. London, the President of the Hotel Division, took responsibility for all the general managers and their assistants. Insisting that everyone comply with the demanding work schedule originated from his European background and training. Openly berating Jitters at the top of his lungs in front of everyone publicly embarrassing him to make a point, set the tone for everyone. The only point he attempted to make was that he demanded respect and all the servers should fall in line. Real communication, between Japes and Mr. London was limited to a single encounter when Mr. London for no reason decided to raise his voice at Japes. Japes, in a calm manner, directed Mr. London to the side of the lobby and said loud enough for any server to hear, "Take your condescending attitude and leave, I don't know who you think you are but you will never talk to me in that fashion!" Mr. London never addressed Japes again.

Shortly after Japes had started in his new position he sampled a taste of the chaos, which, for the next two years, would be his life. Arriving at the hotel early one Monday morning, he beheld over three hundred teenage patrons in the lobby. Maximum capacity for the lobby was maybe fifty. In their infinite wisdom, sales decided to book a student convention of over one thousand for a two-day academic event. Not only did the hotel not have the capacity for such an event the room rate, ridiculously low, yielded no profit. The young guests upset every true customer and Shorty found it necessary to refund over twenty thousand dollars in charges. Japes thought apparently this is why I am here. Jitters, the manager over the weekend, did not even bother to inform Japes or Shorty of the calamity. They both were in shock when they arrived at the mob scene in the lobby.

This group proved to be the tipping point for the front office manager, not only upset as a result of Japes authority, but the relentless beating and sheer pressure the desk was put under grew too much for the server to bear. Also, at this time, Shorty received a promotion to President of the Hotel Division. Apparently Mr. Harsh became disenchanted with the London leadership and prepared to make some big changes for the future of his hotels. Perhaps if Japes wanted to get a promotion, he simply would need to make a twenty thousand dollar boo boo. Timing trumps everything as Japes promoted All-in to be the front office manager and provided the server all the help and support he would need. At their first meeting, Japes showed All-in a centerfold picture of Playboy. He informed All-in that a number of the front office servers would certainly leave as they were close friends with Ron. He would not be too distraught if any boys he hired liked looking at this picture. I know this is not the way to judge a server, but we need a lot of change in attitudes. All-in smiled from ear to ear and said to Japes "I think I am going to try and hire servers who look like this picture". Japes said "Well, there's certainly nothing wrong with that either ". A breath of fresh air came over the front office. Over the next few weeks his personality rubbed off on the new servers and his simple goal focused on keeping the guests and desk servers happy. He never jumped over the desk again.

Now that Jitters took charge the organization eroded into a free-for-all for executives and workers. Jitters went through the motions of being a manager, he conducted the staff meetings, he attended the luncheons, he made the cursory rounds to the departments, but he did not have a clue. He spent most of his time on the telephone asking Shorty what did he want him to do. During this period, Japes and other managers were faced with a dramatic life-and-death situation. An emergency call received at the desk stated that a hotel guest lay face down outside his guest room. Upon arriving at the scene, Japes and his coworkers realized that the man looked blue, and that he was not breathing. They performed CPR as they had been instructed, and while doing so Japes yelled the man was not getting any air into his lungs. When the paramedics jumped in Japes immediately told them something appeared wrong with the airway and CPR did not help. The paramedic summarily dismissed Japes and his coworkers and instructed them to let the pros do the work. After speaking directly to the hospital the paramedic finally inserted a tube far enough down the man's throat to give him air. Later Japes discovered the poor man suffered from a collapsed trachea as a result of surgery months earlier. If the paramedics performed a simple tracheotomy the man would have gotten oxygen. In the end, the guest lost his life and to this day Japes regrets not doing more.

The Harsh Hotels were on the hunt for sales executives as they planned for future expansion. Japes hooked up his old buddy Sot with an interview at one of the hotels. It would be a massive change for him, and would help his family gain financial security. By all reports Sot kept his nose clean and the hotel received recognition for a number of record-breaking years. Sot could sell with the best of them, and the two kept in close touch as they now lived in the greater Cod City area.

Japes spent an inordinate amount of time with Sergey in the housekeeping department. Sergey oversaw a number of head turning female supervisors they were all attractive and caught Japes fancy. Now that Japes held an executive role, he surmised romance with a subordinate would be inappropriate, so there would be no hanky panky, but he spent many fruitful working hours in the girl's company helping make their lives fun. A union in a hotel represented the most ridiculous obstruction to success Japes had ever seen. Unions for servers were marginally necessary many years ago as the Bulls abused workers and paid terrible wages. Hotel work, for the housekeeping department, entailed endless routine, and although it involved hard physical work when one became proficient, it proved rewarding. These servers paid a low-wage, and deserving every penny they made, could not afford the extra monies the union took in dues. It made no sense to Japes at that hotel or any hotel he would work at in the future. In fact, the maintenance and front office departments chose not to join the union realizing the only ones who benefited from the union were the union reps themselves.

The hotel, poorly organized, resulted in situations when the housekeeping department did not have enough linen to make up guest rooms. The housekeeping staff, especially the maids, would leave at a specific time. Japes and All-in on a few occasions would join Sergey and her assistants to strip and clean many guest rooms to accommodate new arrivals. Like most with physical challenges Japes would grin and bear it, always trying to fit in with the team. The hotel was not understaffed it simply did not have the infrastructure to handle the business. Purchasing new equipment would solve the problem, but many years would pass before approving the obvious.

After one such exhausting night All-in, Japes, and the girls felt it necessary to partake in a thirsty Thursday libation. The mall across the street, home to a nice bar, frequented regularly by many of the hotel servers acted as their watering hole. Working hard and drinking was second nature for this gang. One of the assistants, Katie, showed a particular liking for All-in. All-in, unattached, and a popular server with many of the ladies grew up in the general area and visited all the hot spots. After leaving the fine drinking establishment, Katie informed the group that she felt so amorous she could hardly contain herself. Upon hearing this unsolicited declaration, Japes jaw hit the proverbial floor and he scurried home as fast as he could. Only All-in would know what transpired that evening. As hard as everybody worked it felt necessary to let off the stress in some fashion. Everyone did it in different ways, but Japes found that drinking proved by far to be the most common denominator amongst servers.

When Jitters received a promotion to general manager the company replaced him with a new server named Capes, who appeared to be the spitting image of Ricky Nelson. Capes had the ability to persuade, but most importantly, he proved to be a rare normal server with whom Japes would collaborate throughout his hotel career. To Japes, a normal server represented someone who could have thrived in many different fields. Capes fit right in, extremely disciplined and familiar with hotel operations, he brought organization to the food and beverage department, and in the long run became a general manager himself. Although his time at the hotel would not be long the changes he implemented were carried on for many years after he left. Japes and Capes worked well together as they shared similar values basically giving Japes little direction and letting him do his thing. Capes, more than anything, would turn out to be a model family man. This is beyond rare for the nomad world of most servers, and drew the two together with a similar perspective on time. Although he worked hard at the beginning of his career, the priority would always remain with his family. "We work to live, we don not live to work" would be an appropriate outlook for a successful server.

At this time, the company increased the number of executives at all the hotels. Schaffer was hired as the first food and beverage director that the castle ever employed. A flamboyant character with a big flair for the dramatic, meticulous with the details, he oversaw all the bars and food outlets. He and his friend Guy, the reservation manager, were lovers. Keeping their private lives hidden from the hotel staff proved impossible. Japes related well with Schaffer and Guy, as they both were true masters at helping guests. The server masses, however, were not so kind when they dismantled their personal lives. Guy would survive the onslaught of prejudice and ignorance put forth by many of the servers, but Schaffer would not be so lucky. Disenchanted with his role at the hotel, he started to disconnect. One of his greatest responsibilities involved taking care of the Sunday brunch, as the hotel served well over one thousand guests every Sunday afternoon; it was a big production, which required meticulous planning and hard work for a four-hour period. One Sunday Capes was checking the weekend brunch and realized nothing had been prepared and guests were already arriving. He quickly got the ball rolling and after some delay managed to put out the well attended, Sunday brunch. As he walked back to his office, he could hear a piano being played in the nightclub. The nightclub, closed to the public, had been unlocked and when he opened the door, he witnessed a grinning Schaffer, playing to his heart's content. It would be Schaffer's last day at the hotel. Servers can be cruel and this tough crowd proved too much to deal with. Schaffer went on to become a famous composer who to this day composes and lives in a beautiful apartment on Park Avenue in the Empire City. He found his true world and brought joy to thousands.

Mr. Harsh rolled out a plan which surprised even Japes. One morning the big announcement spread throughout the company, he had purchased ten more hotels. Realizing there were only four hotels in the portfolio at the time, the common belief amongst the executives was that the company had recruited to manage their existing properties in a more professional and efficient manner, not to staff new hotels. No change in philosophy or commitment to success motivated ownership, they essentially stumbled into a simple numbers game and a half ass plan to prepare for a historical expansion, and soon the changes began. Within a two-month period, Jitters transferred to Ocean City, All-in transferred to Ocean City, Capes transferred to a neighboring town, Shorty "got the axe" from Mr. Harsh, and a new player named Fitz became the hotel manager. So much for a slow progression, it would suddenly become an extremely stressful time for all the servers. The only two executives who remained, Japes and Classee, were left to deal with the chaos, which shortly ensued.

Of course Japes friend All-in had to be given a world-class send off. All-in received a promotion to the same position that Japes held in a sparkling new fifty million dollar hotel. A formidable challenge for All-in, but, after a short period of time, he achieved the first steps in a successful career. "What would you like to do on your last day with the hotel"? Asked Japes. "Well, I don't know for sure, but let us have a few drinks I think!" replied All-in. And so they did. To this day, Japes, cannot recall or even put together the events that lead to All-in's departure, remembering only they consumed many cocktails with umbrellas and devoured Asian food at two in the morning. Not sure what they did for the other eight hours, All-in, simply claimed, it was the best send off he could have hoped for.

During the past two years All-in and Japes did plenty of carousing at various events around Cod City and even a few road trips. All-in had many friends in the area and introduced Japes to them at parties, fairs, sporting events, and on the golf course. All-in loved to gamble so on one crazy "road trip" Japes, All-in, and a few of his cronies went to an NBA game in the Empire City. After a few beers the group left the arena while celebrating their hometown team's victory. As luck would have it there was a racetrack adjacent to the stadium and if they hurried they could make a wager or two. The race featured trotters something Japes never bet on. Well, it came down to the final race and All-in said to

Japes, " How much cash do you have?" " I have forty dollars left." he replied. " Good I have sixty dollars, give me your forty I'm putting it all on number ten. I know this horse and it is going off at ten to one," declared All-in. Japes and the gang stood at the bar with twenty ounce cups of beer cheering on their horse to a narrow victory! They just won one thousand dollars or so they thought. During the photo finish review, the judges determined that the rider for horse number ten used his whip to hit another horse thus resulting in a disqualification. Flailing his arm against his beer cup in one fell swoop, he completely drenched the man next to him. By some miracle the group escaped without a scratch as the sympathetic man told them in thirty years of betting at that track he had never seen a horse disqualified for that offense. Japes would miss All-in, but something told him this would not be the last meeting between the two nomad servers.

The Holiday season had arrived, when these big changes took place, and Mr. Harsh insisted the managers enjoy a tremendous Christmas party, so he opened up the purse strings and hired an entertainment company. The ballroom, filled with racks of lamb, tenderloins of beef, and virtually every fine bit of cuisine a server could imagine elevated the venue. The ice carvings were shaped with little toboggan runs and drinks of choice were poured for shooters. Caviar hand delivered to each and every attendee, while Mr. Harsh pleaded with Japes to start dancing with the beautiful servers at the party; he wanted nothing but positive comments. A room full of hotel servers with unlimited food and beverage presented quite the scene. It proved unnecessary for Mr. Harsh to motivate the crowd, they did quite fine on their own. None of the servers were permitted to drive home that evening, and in fact most found it difficult simply making it to their guest room. Rumored that many of the attendees woke up in beds with romantic partners for that night only fueled the office gossip. Killer, in particular, seemed to have made the rounds to a number of different rooms. The next day brought mind numbing hangovers and a tremendous rush for the bloody merry mix. It became a tradition with this particular group to have a little bit of the hair of the dog that bit them. No one knows if any little servers were conceived that night, but it surely highlighted a holiday season to remember.

Fitzy, was only there on a temporary basis and the new manager, Darken soon arrived. An English Bull, recently arriving in the country a few weeks prior, he comported himself with a limited amount of energy, totally set in his ways. Reluctantly, he dealt with a few executives in the hotel, and would not even address the staff or managers, as his schedule had him arriving later than most managers and leaving promptly at five o'clock every day. Realizing that Japes knew everybody in the hotel, he randomly took tours of the property with him by his side. Summoning Japes to his office and telling him that they were going on a walkabout evolved into a routine. Two types of walkabouts', one on the outside of the hotel and one on the inside of the hotel, completed his day. These were the times when he executed all of his managing, and he funneled directives through Japes. If there were any issues with a female employee Darken coached Japes, "Why don't you just throw a leg over her and solve the issue." Japes, the first time he heard this "request", assumed he must be joking, however, after he repeated the expression every other day Japes realized he was serious. Darken, in an executive meeting, referred to a number of servers as spics. Well, the HR department got wind of these comments and it was not long before the corporate office found out. Abruptly escorted off the property after two months of service, there would be no more walkabouts' for old Darken. This boondoggle perpetuated the long line of poorly thought out decisions implemented by the Harsh Company.

One of the true highlights of this world for Japes involved a beautiful bell server by the name of Sarah. Sarah made an incredible first impression with her beautiful smile and gorgeous blonde hair cascading down her shoulders. She dressed the same as the boys in an immaculate beefeater outfit that fit her like a glove. It was the only time in Japes career and in his travels, that he worked with or even saw a female bell server. Customers became so attached to

Sarah that they would ask for her upon arrival if they did not see her in the lobby. The guests themselves would help load the luggage onto the bell carts and push the cart down the hallways with her. A rather petite server, she, however, carried her own weight, and efficiently performed all of the duties that the boys could handle. Qualities of her daily interactions were hard to define, as she not only projected a great presence, but her engagement with guests and staff alike, felt as though she stood performing on a stage. Of course, being on the stage is what all good servers tried to do. Sarah, however, did it so naturally that it made her incredibly approachable by all. It turned out that Sarah was a full-time student at a school of art in the city, and her vocation, her true passion in life, involved singing in the opera. Most of the singers Japes had seen in the opera were big with robust and incredible voices. Well, Sarah sang with the best of them, and she would eventually become an opera star performing on stages all over the world. Japes fascinated that someone, who would later become so successful as an opera singer, could truly thrive in the hotel world. Her tips on average were double the other bell servers simply because of her disposition and ability to make guests happy. He did not believe any correlation between the arts and the hotel existed until Sarah came along. Japes came to realize that taking care of a server's needs was as much an art form as it was a task. You cannot teach a server about the nuances of giving, and although there would never be anything definitive about this feeling, Japes knew that art lived in almost all vocations, especially those involving personal interactions.

Mack and the executive administrator Hot-hips were quite the item. Although Mack was fifteen years older than Hot-hips, they were an item. A proud server with a great passion for the ocean, he loved to go boating where he and Hot-hips spent many a summer day out on the boat. Fishing and drinking beer, while Hot-hips bathed in the sun, occupied the warm summer days. Mack introduced Japes to the pleasures of boating in the ocean. He recognized Japes physical limitations and artfully demonstrated the least strenuous avenues to take, while maintaining a boat. The yacht club acted as much like a summer vacation home as any Japes experienced. Mack and Hot-hips were not married and they dated for nearly twenty years. Japes would remain friends with his boating companions for the rest of his life. It evolved into one of the few extensions from the workplace, which turned into a true passion, and for that Japes would always be grateful.

The infamous health club, under Japes umbrella of authority, spotlighted the ugly politics with this group. After many years of service, Maggie decided to retire as the director. Mr. Harsh and his wife had grown fond of her and expected any new manager to do literally the same as she had done. Well, obviously no two servers are exactly the same, but Japes did his best to fulfill the needs of all the health club members especially Mr. and Mrs. Harsh. Betty, Maggie's assistant, had worked in the health club for a couple of years was a beautiful server, professionally trained and well respected by the staff. After much consideration, Japes promoted Betty to the director's position in the health club. He coached Betty before he promoted her on how to interact with the owners. Some time had passed and all things appeared to be going well at the club. Mack, directly connected to the corporate staff, heard rumors that there were problems in the health club requiring immediate attention. What could possibly be wrong in the health club thought Japes. The memberships were up, the health department satisfied, and even the temperature of the pool remained exactly as the Harsh's demanded. Japes and Mack were both perplexed. Sitting behind his desk contemplating life one day, the inevitable call from the corporate office finally came. Told in no uncertain terms that he must terminate Betty, and there would be no discussion, he complied. Mrs. Harsh did not like her. She did not like her when she was the assistant and it had nothing to do with her current job performance. In fact, Betty performed better as a director than Maggie, and Maggie directed the club for twenty-five years. It broke Japes heart to tell Betty that she would no longer be in charge of the health club. He could not even give her a good reason other than some bullshit story the corporate office invented.

The waters in the world at the castle suddenly became very murky. Japes had been in the world for only twenty-five months, but it seemed like twenty-five years. Working for five managers in this brief period, and seeing more servers come and go during that time than he did in his entire career exhausted him. Forced in the end to fire a server for absolutely no cause felt both ridiculous and hurtful. He had become disenchanted with the business in general and in particular with his inability to stand up for a fellow server, he therefore resigned his position effective immediately. He knew all worlds were not like this, but he also knew some serious soul-searching lay ahead to decide his future. Japes understood that all people possess the same amount of time, but how one spends their time and the rewards recognized for that commitment mattered the most. How could he be sure that the next world would be better or could it even be worse? Well, isn't that the mystery thought Japes. He felt he failed, although he had not. The Harsh world, never clear enough to thrive in, abruptly came into perspective when Japes learned of his father's passing. Suddenly, this great calamity became totally insignificant. His dad's philosophy and Japes upbringing would forever overcome these mere curiosities.

THE OASIS

Becoming a suburban server, and remaining in the same geographical area had come to fruition. After taking time off to collect his thoughts and mourn the loss of his father, he arrived at the new hotel pleasantly surprised by the beauty of the lobby. The interior reminded him of the hotel in the Mountain City, as it displayed an open atrium with beautiful plantings spread throughout. The lobby itself contained an open-air restaurant, an enclosed fine dining restaurant, and an elevated lobby bar. The overall layout, somewhat smaller than the Mountain City hotel, appeared well appointed and showed nicely. This would be the first time Japes accepted a position through a "headhunter", as recruiters were notorious for simply filling slots and not necessarily with good organizations. Japes built a rapport with this particular headhunter, and hoped he would not steer him in the wrong direction. In fact, he took a tour of the general area and discovered it to be quite nice; this suburban property, surrounded by malls, corporations, and over one hundred restaurants, seemed to be ideal. The group of towns, which made this area quite attractive not only for its location, but its infrastructure, enjoyed constant traffic. The area boasted three of the most affluent towns in the entire state, with a State University located less than three miles away. Japes first impression, after meeting with his boss, was that this might be the nicest world he had ever seen.

Duffer, the general manager, an influential server, hailing from the Flatlands area of the country, had been recruited for his extensive background in the hotel Industry; he enjoyed no ties to the community, inherited a poorly, managed beautiful property leaving him with nothing but upside. Looking like the pink panther on steroids with his long droopy face and saggy ears, Duffer's true passion outweighed the rigors of managing the hotel. A scratch golfer, he manipulated his schedule enabling him to play a round of golf at any time. An odd situation, but Japes, not arguing the point, played dozens of rounds of golf with him over the next twelve months, and despite Japes progressive loss of muscle, Duffer would make him a better player.

Japes inherited some departments that were in total disarray. The health-club, essentially just a pool, managed by two physical education students who showed up and left whenever they felt like it, not only left the hotel exposed to major liability, it broke all local regulations. Tidy, a man who had never before worked in a hotel, managed the maintenance department, logging a mere thirty hours per week and never coming in on the weekends. His staff followed in his footsteps and pretty much did whatever they felt like. The housekeeping manager, Pillows, a thirty-year veteran, knew what to do, but personified a career Kiva. The guest rooms would only be cleaned to the proper standard when pressure was applied to her and her staff. The front office, the central hub of the hotel, employed no manager. The company believed that this area should be run with three supervisors, and they would equally share the responsibilities of the department. An organizational calamity, which for the next fifteen years, Japes gladly defended. He would organize it the way he wanted and let the cards fall where they may.

Duffer, a strange dude, although knowledgeable about the business he did not implement any changes to the hotel. Japes, early on, realized that Duffer would not stay for any length of time; he acted like a typical hotelier moving every two or three years. Japes, cognizant of how clear the waters were in this particular world, made the decision to do all he could to make it a success. The one ingredient remaining at the forefront of his oversight, involved the hierarchy of the hotel, not only the owners, but also the executives who dealt with the owners. The relationship with both the staff and the community greatly depended on this critical hierarchy. After getting an understanding of what needed to be done, Japes attended his first monthly meeting at the corporate offices. This monthly meeting would forever be called "the wood shed meeting". Held every month to review both the financial situation of the hotel, and receive any directives set forth by the Grand Poobah, evolved into a ritual. The executive, Scam was an unusual tiny little thing. A bully, who looked like the Penguin from the Batman series, he demonstrated many undesirable characteristics while ruling over his dominion. He established no personal relationships with anyone, he displayed odious traits, and he appeared to be a taker amongst givers. The good news, he demonstrated little intelligence and his sole purpose in the world revolved around maintaining his executive position. He never followed up on any directives and spent all of his time dealing with ownership. This arrangement would work in Japes and the hotel's favor for more than a decade.

Since Duffer spent little time correcting the issues at the hotel and worrying mainly about where he would play his next round of golf, Japes decided to set up a good organization. The first challenge he uncovered involved something that he did not like. The lead night auditor, Simon, had a terrible reputation for showing up late and not completing the audit on time. To compound this problem, there were many evenings when Simon worked as the only night auditor. During his first month at the hotel, Japes regularly received calls in the middle of the night by a disgruntled supervisor. When starting from scratch the only way to correct an issue involved observation and uncovering everything one could by seeing it directly. He would come into the hotel unannounced at two in the morning to see what was going on. Unfortunately, the rumors about the behavior of Simon were accurate. Japes would often find Simon pickled out of his mind with his breath stinking of whiskey. In fact, one morning he arrived early only to find Simon asleep in the bell closet, using luggage as his pillow. Not only did Simon turn in his work late it was also inaccurate. The hotels financial reporting's for the past two years were not even close to being correct, as this poor alcoholic Flathead had been left to his own devices. Whose fault was this? Japes did not want to be the heavy he just wanted to do the best he could. Simon had a disease and he deserved to be treated with respect. In fact, Japes did not do anything in persuading Simon to change his behavior. After a few visits during Simon's shift and the realization that he would be required to actually do a proper job he never returned to the hotel.

Japes recruited a server named Casanova. Casanova, a skinny influential server who worked for many years as a desk manager for various hotel chains, appeared unusually jumpy and continuously smoked a cigarette. Although Japes did not have a desk manager position he needed someone to clean up the mess on the overnight shift. Casanova not only cleaned up the overnight shift, he hired an assistant named Parka. Parka, a true Flathead, to the dismay of all front office servers refused to wear a bra. If this lack of undergarment turned out to be the only issue that Japes would encounter on the overnight shift well he, with a little tact, would appease the befuddled masses. Casanova also loved his drugs and booze, but had enough sense never to come to the hotel pickled. He had a bad habit of flicking the ashes from his cigarette onto the shoes of people he did not like. Eventually they would come to an understanding over this bizarre habit. So for the next ten years either Parka or Casanova would take care of the overnight shift. Japes encountered virtually no late night issues and nurtured a great relationship with the auditors. Some just did not realize how important this shift affected the management of a hotel. They had limited resources and would often make important decisions, decisions for everyones' safety and for the business in general. For this peace of mind Japes felt eternally grateful.

The true challenge to the hotel centered in the front office, as it was not possible to have three servers responsible for one area. Japes knew, after some observation, that his area of expertise remained dysfunctional and had been supported by Duffer and Scam for supposedly financial reasons. Japes thought long and hard as to why the business, which took in millions of dollars, would try and save a few hundred dollars a year in salary. This decision in reality cost the owners much more in lost revenues. A desk manager would easily have found out the inaccuracy of the financial reporting and all the other shortfalls. There were three attractive servers in charge of the desk. Holly, Molly, and Polly were young, influential supervisors who took on separate roles and basically worked at the desk. They were incompetent, but Japes discovered why all three were there. They were all quite the callipygians', and had been approved of by Scam. Japes, in his way, made each accountable for certain activities in the front office. When one has not been accountable for years they do not take change well. It did not take long for Holly, Molly and Polly to realize that they were takers, not givers, and much to Scam's chagrin they would need to find a new gig. Duffer told Japes to hire new supervisors and Japes informed him that he would only be hiring one. "I'm not going to spend any more money than we have budgeted this year, but I'm going to hire a front office manager and make them accountable. A supervisor will work for this manager and we will have a responsible server twenty four hours a day," stated Japes.

Japes immediately promoted Casanova to the first front office manager ever hired at the hotel. It is what Casanova wanted to begin with and enabled Japes to establish continuity and communication on a full time basis. Casanova did, however, have to compromise on his cigarette smoking. He and Japes came to the agreement that he would chew tobacco instead of smoke. Done in a discrete manner he continued to get away with this sketchy habit for an extended period of time. Casanova hired good servers and represented the hotel well. He would occasionally bring Japes to tears when telling him about his escapades. He particularly liked the ladies and would mention getting his carrot buttered on a regular basis. It took Japes a few times to figure out exactly what Casanova muttered. Japes thought, he must feel comfortable around him to reveal such intimate adventures.

The health club was the next item on Japes radar. Extremely concerned with the fact that these two knuckleheads came and went whenever they felt like it, leaving guests unattended, demanded change. Lumpy and Stumpy were college students who played on the football team. They did not have an ounce of common sense between the two of them. Whenever Japes had a chance to check on the health club, they were either sitting in the sauna or sitting in the hot tub. As this was a quiet club, oftentimes there would be no patrons swimming. Japes did not mind if they wanted to do their homework, but they were required to sit at the counter and keep an eye on the club. He thought this to be the easiest job that two college students could possibly have. The two clowns could not even do that, resulting in the quickest and easiest decision Japes ever made. He fired both of them, closed the club, and hired a manager with the responsibility of finding some local memberships. The pool, perfectly designed for light water aerobics, attracted the senior crowd for local memberships, and Japes sole instruction was to never leave the club unattended. We would rather have upset guests than dead ones. He could not quite think why Duffer had not done this himself, but for lack of caring.

The maintenance department, managed by a knowledgeable man who for many years labored as a foreman in a manufacturing plant, stood in complete disarray. He possessed an understanding of mechanical devices, but displayed no skills of management or customer service. Tidy previously worked in a union and so he expected to take long breaks and have two servers to do the job of one. The Oasis, only 2 years old, displayed few, if any, mechanical problems, and it would be years before major and even minor mechanical issues would arise. The hotel, relatively small in comparison to a number of hotels Japes previously worked in, contained two hundred and fifty guest rooms in a tower section. The main facility, especially the kitchen, looked quite small. However, the well laid out design utilized every square inch of space for either the guests or the staff. Tidy, a roomy server, quite tall, who wore glasses, always meandered about the facility with his assistant by his side morning, noon, and night. The two were inseparable and came to be known as "Laurel and Hardy." The hotel needed a maintenance server sixteen hours a day, and Tidy would not agree to these hours, especially on the weekends. He did not think his department needed to be on the property and his staff should be able to take the weekends off for recreation. Japes, faced with the reality that another department had never been managed and did whatever it wanted needed to take action. No wonder Duffer enjoyed a great golf game he sure did not spend any time managing the hotel.

After several meetings and discussions with Tidy, Japes realized that it was a lost cause. He respected him for his knowledge, Tidy, however, was not going to change his schedule for anyone whether it was in the best interest of the hotel or not. Fortunately, Japes recruited a new engineer who worked in hotels for a number of years, and this transition occurred in a civil manner. Tidy, resigned his position and pursued a more conventional career, while the new engineer, Waldo, turned out to be quite a character. An outgoing server, somewhat unusual for the position, he arrived with strong recommendations and a working knowledge of all the trades. He did not appear to be a leader, but more a glorified supervisor, and brandishing Brown Nose traits were nipped in the bud, as this would get him nowhere. His round jolly face would pop up all over the hotel as he got his staff to actually do some work. This area of the hotel would be a work in progress, but Japes wanted to see what Waldo could do.

Duffer would hang around the world for about a year, as Japes diligently worked in his areas of responsibility to make a good foundation for service to the thousands of guests who would stay at their hotel, Duffer realized he could use Japes connections. The hotel did over three million dollars in food and beverage sales every year. The catering department did the bulk of these sales. The catering director, like most of the other department managers, had been positioned over his head. Japes, called his buddy Capes from the Castle Hotel to come and be the director of catering. Japes assured Duffer that he would have no problems in this department if he hired Capes. He would organize the sales office and he would organize the operations team. This is what he did, and Capes stayed in that position for twenty years. Capes and his family represented a rare commodity in the world of servers. It takes a certain discipline and a worldly perspective to balance the rewards of being a true server and a parent. The Capes family lived in an affluent community and by most standards lived a 'normal' life. Capes was not old school and would dedicate only part of his time to the Hotel. Whether it be coaching his children's sports teams or tending to real estate investments Capes remained balanced. This philosophy contradicted the norm, as being a server entailed a lifelong commitment, which usually required most of ones' time. Everyone, however, learned that time spent serving did not have to be all encompassing. In fact, one could see the trees despite the forest with a clearer mind and a balanced commitment. This presented a dichotomy for some of the team to be sure, but a productive contribution, and a cornerstone to the successful culture.

Events during Capes years at the Hotel included a managers' retreat to his home for a day of fun. The team, one summer day, met at a marina near his home and boarded a pontoon boat for an excursion down river. The team picnicked on shrimp cocktail and tea sandwiches while viewing the beautiful scenery. Back at the home they all participated in a whiffle ball hitting contest and various yard games. He had been "server extraordinaire," that day, and demonstrated his skills to those who questioned his commitment.

The hotel, at this time, also employed a full-time purchaser. The jumpy little character who acted in this position was a glorified dishwasher. He had no understanding of what a purchaser actually did. He simply unloaded the trucks and made sure the boxes of produce matched the invoices. Japes brought in another server from the Castle Hotel, Elko the purchaser with whom he had worked, believing him to be the best server for the job. He would save the hotel thousands of dollars, particularly in the area of food and beverage. He brought in a sense of humor, which amused the staff and built camaraderie. Of all the servers Japes worked with, Elko enjoyed the driest sense of humor of any. A good golfer, although he did have an eraser on his golf pencil, he would prove to be another partner for the Duffer golf outings.

Elko had the longest commute of anyone with well over a two-hour daily ride, and displayed a unique personality one could not categorize. The one-story, which summed up Elko, left a number of the staff peeing their pants they laughed so hard. One day Elko came walking into the office wearing a very large pair of loafers. Japes looked at his feet and said "New pair of shoes Elko?" "No, not exactly said Elko" "what do you mean?" inquired Japes. "Well, on my way to work this morning, and almost halfway to the hotel, I realized my shoes had this terrible rip down the side and a hole in the soul. I looked out my car window and spotted a pair of shoes in a driveway. I stopped my car went over and took the shoes. The shoes are a little too big, but they are better than what I had." stated Elko. Japes thought you can't even dream these things up who in their right mind would stop and take a pair of shoes off of someone's driveway. And so, Elko walked around with shoes big enough for a clown bragging about the free pair he found. What kind of server was he?

As springtime approached in Japes first year at the Oasis, he and Duffer were summoned by the owners to their flagship hotel in the heart of the South. Japes and Duffer had never been to this part of the country before. They were wined and dined and shown about the town by the flamboyant general manager of the Somebody Hotel. The purpose of the trip was to impress the two managers as to the families' wealth and to spread the word what great owners they were. At sundown, they even held a dance on the rooftop of this historic hotel. There were nearly one hundred patrons dancing, eating hors d'oeuvres, and drinking cocktails until two in the morning. Japes and Duffer were impressed. The mission was accomplished, as Japes spread the word to all that the family owned half a city block in the downtown area, and the hotel division comprised less than five percent of their real estate portfolio. Furthermore, the family, the largest landowner in the state, took in more than two billion dollars in revenues each year. Japes knew from his experience that working for owners with deep pockets, greatly improved that chances for success. He also knew, it felt fantastic not to have to work at the flagship hotel and deal with all the individual needs of the hierarchy.

Golf became such a priority to Duffer that it consumed a large part of the hotel's weekly plan. Japes and Elko were asked to play golf at least two times per week. The first round of golf, at a nice public golf course, told Japes a lot about Duffer. Duffer, a scratch golfer, on this long, difficult course shot an even par seventy-two. His nickname from the mini tour, "The Knife", characterized his ability to strike a one-iron further than most could hit a driver. He hit the ball long, he hit the ball straight, he could putt, and he hated to lose. Of course, being a scratch golfer, he always wanted to play for money. So Japes and Elko not only came up with cash to play the round, but cash to pay every time they lost. To compound the situation, Elko and Japes liked to walk the golf course, but they were forced to chip in for a golf cart, as Duffer owned an enormous professional golf bag. The bag weighed nearly 50 pounds so nobody would have carried it around the golf course. Japes thought this too good to be true even if he ran the risk of going broke. Something would have to give either at work or on the golf course.

As Duffer felt more and more pressure from Scam over the performance of the hotel, he played more and more golf. The realization that Scam would never have any interpersonal relationship with him drove him away from work. The memos became nastier and nastier, but there was never any follow up. To appease Duffer, as Japes simply lacked the necessary golf skills, he arranged for some matches with his friends. Duffer won every match Japes set up for him and he got him onto some of the best golf courses around the city. He set him up against Millsy, his college roommate, who played a skilled game. They played at Millsy's home course and Japes was damned if Duffer didn't shoot par and win again. The situation became insufferable, and a little too much for Japes to bear resulting in a true competitive match. Duffer played against a golfer nicknamed, "The Bull", at an exclusive private country club. The Bull, coincidentally a bull in life, was Millsy's brother, and a professional golfer. The group, halfway through the round, and Duffer getting his butt kicked, stopped as he complained of a sore back, eventually insisting he would struggle through the pain. He lost every way he could to the Bull and reluctantly paid off his bets. Finally, it punctuated the end of Duffers constant bragging and egotistical demeanor. They actually spent more time at the hotel doing what they were supposed to. Japes eternally grateful as he could not afford to keep playing this much golf, and he had run out of golfing buddies for Duffer to challenge.

Duffer's time at the hotel came to an end, a knowledgeable server to be sure, but for whatever reason he did not choose to apply his skills. He did as little as possible to get by and never made a real commitment to improving the business. Most of the management and staff at the hotel felt little appreciation towards Duffer. The good servers of the Oasis, however, wanted to give Duffer a nice send off. The hotel sponsored a party for Duffer at a nearby drinking establishment. All of the managers and many of the line staff came to wish Duffer and his family great success. Duffer decided to transfer back to the Flatlands with his pregnant wife and daughter. His true passion would push him to a different region, and a different type of hotel in the heart of golf country. At the party all the servers were surprised when the future general manager's girlfriend decided to attend.

She worked at the corporate office, but had little dealings with the hotel itself. As the night wore on Duffer, Elko, Japes, and the night manager returned to the hotel to have a nightcap. Well, Duffer showed the gang his true colors by escorting the future manager's girlfriend into a guest room for a romantic interlude. He left with about as much class as he had shown to his current hotel family. In the years to follow Elko would often whisper to Japes "Doesn't Bootlick's son look a lot like Duffer?" Bootlick was the new G.M. This marked the beginning of the mud to be introduced to this beautiful crystal clear world.

A New Era

Bootlick, a unique creature to inhabit the hotel world, had been born entirely brown as opposed to the run of the mill Kiva displaying just a brown nose, thus bestowing upon him the ability to be completely superficial. Knowing only the periphery in managing a hotel and like Scam solely interested in maintaining his position for as long as he could, uniquely qualified him for a single duty. His task for the next ten years would be to keep Scam and the powers to be away from the hotel, and would be considered the poster boy for the entire region as he ran the flagship property in the northeast territory. He did, however, introduce politics and deceit to the hotel culture. Along with Bootlick, the country embraced eight years of Clinton and the ensuing economic boom. Fortunately, the existing management and the incredible staff were well prepared to carry the Hotel to new unimagined heights. The culture dictated that any important event or decision that affected the guest would never be brought to Bootlick's attention. Every time Bootlick became involved in an operational or strategic decision it turned into a calamity and the wrong decision would be made. The "very" general manager did like his wine and he managed with such a laissez-faire attitude that the team remained happy and productive. The groundwork was now set not only for the management of the hotel but also for the profitability of the business. The hotel had never performed to its potential, although the area thrived with many different companies all of which utilized hotel services for their business. The affluent neighboring towns were ripe for solicitation to the beautiful banquet facilities. The potential for real growth had been right in front of everybody's nose and the gang would make it happen.

Japes needed to make a few key changes before the hotel could take off. Hotels make money by putting heads in beds. The demand for the beds at the Oasis was much greater than the owners and executives realized. Japes searched for a reservation manager to work as an ally in making the business some real money. Seems stood out as Japes choice to manage the intricacies of filling the hotel at the highest possible rate. An intelligent server with a great willingness to please, her demeanor fit in well with the other servers at the hotel and she enjoyed the culture afforded her. Seems, born a mentsch, similar to the owner Japes worked with at camp many years ago, understood the evolving technology as computer skills and yield management programs became the tools of the trade. Japes responsibilities as an executive included making money, he and Seems worked together to fill the hotel by changing the way business had been conducted in the past. There would be less need for group business, and there would be an increased use of transient demand. Over the next decade the hotel would double its average rate and maintain the same percentage of occupied rooms. The business would recognize its full potential with this implementation. It would be accompanied with some key operational changes.

All guests who stay at a hotel form their opinions within the first three minutes of entering. Hoteliers refer to this as "a sense of arrival." The current sense of arrival, at the Oasis, presented an elderly server named Vick who always had doughnut dust smudged on the front of his uniform. He was a wonderful man, however, this glorified van driver showed no skills in dealing with the public. When Japes became familiar with all of the staff at the hotel, he targeted a server working in the maintenance department. Zorro, a handsome older server who moved to the area from a country in the Subcontinent, displayed all the attributes. He worked in the organization for many years as a maintenance man, but Japes encouraged Zorro to make a change in his life and greet every person who entered the hotel. Zorro agreed to take this position and became the first true doorman the hotel ever hired. During the many years that Zorro greeted the guests, management received hundreds of letters complimenting Zorro and his service. One of the best moves the hotel ever made and Japes became convinced that this key decision helped turn the tide to success.

Pepe' Le Fete, a tall, slender, handsome server with a great accent, ruled the banquet department. Born in France, he soon thereafter moved to the U.S., and became an

American citizen. As a leader, he worked hard and managed an effective and happy banquet staff. He earned the respect of all the servers in his area of responsibility, as the team provided a level of service far greater than most hotels of the same caliber. He maintained a wonderful sense of humor, which he employed while motivating the housemen under difficult conditions. The facility was laid out in such a manner whereby the housemen constantly shuffled tables and chairs due to the extreme lack of storage space. Pepe' Le Fete worked directly for Capes and the two servers maintained an interesting relationship. Capes and his assistant would book more business in the hotel than even the owners thought possible. Pepe' Le Fete would graciously service all of these new customers, subsequently the banquet staff earned excellent money from the gratuities, as did Capes from his commissions. Pepe' Le Fete, however, bore the brunt of these additional events, and received only a marginal wage increase for the additional million in sales. He never complained and remained a true cornerstone of management for many years. His success would carry on and lead him to a successful career as a food service executive. Japes hoped during his tenure that Pepe' Le Fete would have been promoted to food and beverage director. He put forth this recommendation, but Bootlick went in another direction. Just one of many mistakes the group would reluctantly overcome through the years.

The sous chef, Toy, a Bull even smaller than Scam, encompassed the culinary area regularly swearing at everyone entering and exiting the kitchen. Emulating a tiny Bull's complex, and although a talented cook, he managed to piss off every server in the hotel. He represented the old school in believing the sous chef should run the hotel's kitchen. Japes, one day walked into the kitchen looking for an item to put in the cafeteria, and Toy, in his infinite wisdom, started swearing at Japes telling him to get the hell out of the kitchen and to stay in some area of the hotel that he had a clue about. Japes said, "You little piece of crap I have forgotten more about kitchens than you will ever know. I will make it my mission to get you out of here entirely if you talk to me in that manner ever again!" Over the years Toy and Japes became friends both inside and outside the hotel. They attended many dinner parties at their homes and shared in the joy of becoming parents for the first time. It's amazing what a little civility can do to one's life. Japes also recommended Toy for a position as the executive chef during his years there. Again, this recommendation would not be used and another poor decision had been made by Bootlick. It punctuated the last recommendation Japes would ever make concerning personnel.

Toy owned a hidden sanctuary where he and his wife would often escape, during the warm summer days. On one occasion he invited Japes and some close friends for a day of adventure and relaxation. The group met Toy early in the morning at a small marina and boarded his skiff taking the short trip across the harbor to a small island. There were a half dozen summer homes on the island each containing its own generator and a few creature comforts. The main means of transportation were old golf carts.

The plan for the day entailed feasting on a low country picnic with baby back ribs and whatever bounty could be harvested from the ocean. Toy placed his ribs on a homemade smoker, which would require a few more hours of cooking to complete. The group changed into their swimwear and walked down to the muddy shore. Clams and scallops appeared everywhere, as each year when the area experienced this exceptionally low tide the ocean's bounty appeared right at their feet. The water receded nearly three feet more than normal. Everyone watched in amazement as Toy, hunched over with both arms under water as if he was searching for an underwater treasure, slowly traversed the shoreline. With his feet he would feel the ocean floor for small holes where lobsters would hide. In one smooth motion, he pushed with one hand into the opening and as the lobster thrust itself backwards, he caught it and placed it in a secured net. He had mastered this highly illegal technique and managed to catch thirty-three lobsters. Japes had never seen or even heard of anything like it. The feast tasted beyond good as both Toy and his wife were excellent cooks with ingredients caught within an hour of eating. It turned out to be quite an adventure and showed everyone as to Toy's ingenuity and survival instincts. He would eventually move on to a successful career as an executive in the world of grub.

Ho-hum, the original chef, and later the food and beverage director had worked at the hotel since day one. There was nothing special about Ho-hum and if he had to be classified Japes would call him a worker. An average cook, but remarkably efficient in managing the kitchen, he inherited an accomplished group of terrific cook's and he did his best to keep them happy. Ho-hum acted unusual in that he was the only person Japes ever met who became quieter the more he drank. Everyone that Japes had ever shared a libation with became more boisterous and more animated as the cocktails continued to flow. Ho-hum, however, became quieter and quieter as he would pound down the beers. There must be some psychological explanation for this, but Japes was at a loss as to why and always thought it to be peculiar. Ho-hum remained pretty much nondescript in his contributions to the hotel and its culture for decades. A follower who complied with whatever Bootlick wanted him to do, he never rocked the boat, he never stood up for any principal, and he never caused any controversy amongst the management. He was, however, the king of kickbacks. All the food and beverage vendors would give gifts to Ho-hum, such as sports tickets, food, and beverage samples. This was a common industry practice, and at one point, Ho-Hum decided to sell sports tickets to fellow servers. This did not represent the true spirit of a team player, especially for a server who made a better living than most. A follower promoted into the role of a leader, he survived the hotel life for many years, and would even be recognized by the company with an award for his efforts. There is something to be said in the hotel world for being a good follower and not rocking the boat. Japes philosophy being, it is not what you say in life that matters, but it is what you do, never applied to Ho-hum. It never applied because he did not initiate anything on his own. He complied with the well-established routines, which during the heyday of the hotel worked just fine he simply followed the pack.

Big Apple was a large server and one of the best cooks in the kitchen. Quite a character, he organized many of the non- work activities throughout the hotel. His accomplishments included the annual Big Apple golf tournament, where all hotel employees could participate awarding prizes to the winners. Big Apple also ran the football pool each year with the winners receiving hundreds of dollars. He ran the Super Bowl extravaganza with significant payouts. Big Apple, for the most part, ran the kitchen in the evening, and earned a reputation for putting together the most expensive tenderloin beef sandwich for a worker in need. Big Apple's skills at cooking were only overshadowed by his contributions to the hotel community at large. He was not without his faults, as no server is perfect. One incident, which came to the attention of management, involved a disruptive staffer. After a number of confrontations, Big Apple had had enough with the incompetence and lack of consideration displayed by this coworker, he made sure during service one of the appetizer plates became exceptionally hot when putting it out for the server to take. Needless to say, the server dropped the plate and screamed at Big Apple for the piping hot dish. Big Apple, in a rather harsh way, made his point and soon thereafter the server left the hotel for another job. When asked what he says to the non-English speaking servers when the plates are hot? Apple said, "I tell them they are damn hot. Everyone must have learned a little English because it works." This portrayed Big Apple at his finest. He has since become one of the best lawyers in the city.

Belly, a lifelong hotelier, worked half his career in the banquet department, and half his career as a room service waiter. Born with the largest bellybutton of anyone Japes had ever seen, Belly, a reformed alcoholic and a confirmed bachelor, spent much of his free time traveling the world. He loved sports, as he was a great athlete in his youth, and frequented many of the professional sporting events. Gaining recognition as a great employee was not in the cards for him, but he and Japes got along just fine. They frequently discussed politics and sports along with many current events. Although smarter than he let on, Belly did not command the respect he deserved by reason of his position. Japes admired his strong will to stop drinking, and looked forward to the discussions regarding various places he traveled to. His favorite story involved Belly's trip to China and the many things he saw. He came back with trinkets including a Chinese Penny ten times the size of an American penny with a hole in the middle. Japes gifted this trinket to his daughter, who to this day cherishes it.

Bo-Bobbie, the executive administrator hired by Bootlick in a hope to keep him organized, miraculously turned out to be the sole personnel decision Bootlick made for the good. Bo-Bobbie, a unique server with skills in many different areas, protected his territory. She remained engaged while attending parties and socializing with people from all different walks of life. Equally comfortable listening to and helping staff with the basic daily requests, she abounded with energy and somehow dealt with Bootlick and his bizarre behavior. She kept in confidence important information and did it all with a fantastic sense of humor. Japes and his wife would spend many an evening partying with Bo-Bobbie and her husband Bo-Bark to the wee hours of the night. Hosting some of the best cocktail parties and social events that Japes would ever attend, Bo-Bobbie and

Japes became lifelong friends, and to this day, even though they live in different parts of the country, they keep in touch. Bo-Bobbie never changed her values and has far exceeded many of Japes peers enjoying a rewarding, successful life.

In the early years the challenge to create a good culture for all the servers proved challenging. Historically, the hotel operated like so many businesses with little time taken to look after and fulfill the needs of the workers. As the commitment changed, and Bootlick deflected the executives away from the property, the productivity and attitudes changed. The communication process became clear to all, as the world transformed into a refreshing, lively environment. The even distribution of resources within the group led to more appropriate participation. The trust in one another grew enough for Casanova to confide in Japes under personal duress. Casanova informed Japes that he would need a leave of absence from the hotel for an extended period of time. He had been convicted of a DUI offense for the second time and in this case he hit a pedestrian with his car. Assigned to "the big house" for as long as one year, he wanted to someday return to his career. Japes, agreed to hire him back to whatever position was available at the time. This promise disregarded all corporate policies, but Japes did not care. Knowing how difficult it had been to find and work with clear thinking positive servers, he committed to remaining loyal to his helpful coworker. When the powers to be found out they would be upset, but they would not have the courage to do anything about it. This bravado proved typical of the executive at the corporate level.

With no one at the helm, the front office fell back into Japes lap. He decided to promote a young college graduate who worked as a supervisor. Bowl, an Influential server with dark rings around his eyes was young for such a position, and he enjoyed smoking pot when not at work. He proved, however, to be excellent with the customers, influential with his coworkers, and motivated an upbeat front office. The pot smoking seemed to be a common occurrence with the front office staff. Japes noticed that the young staff who worked on the weekends all were laid-back and casual. Blinky the part-time operator was a high school student who never missed a day of work. Japes soon figured out that she financed her pot smoking habit by stealing the cash from the coffee cart in the lobby. Guests would leave a dollar in the basket and take a cup of coffee. This honor system had been in place since the hotel opened and enabled the customer to quickly get on their way as they checked out. Japes inevitably said farewell to Blinky, as the entire culture knew she took the money to buy herself pot. Stealing represented something this culture could not tolerate. Wouldn't it be nice if that behavior were not tolerated at the corporate level, thought Japes? He had his doubts after his initial meetings.

To bring the hotel to its potential it needed a new Director of Sales. The current director was shortsighted and did not understand the true economics of the hotel and the marketplace. A young Red-eyed server with a political agenda targeted at preserving her position by discrediting those around her, under many circumstances, would be a formula for success as Japes had seen it before. In this case, however, she targeted Japes himself as being incompetent. She would leave the hotel within two months for the culture changed and the truth prevailed within. She became so disliked as a result of her ridiculous accusations and character assassination, that upon her return from a two-week honeymoon, she found a dead fish inside a package left in her apartment. The home smelled so bad she hired professional cleaners to fumigate. Nobody ever knew who did this, but she apparently overstayed her welcome at the Oasis.

Since Bootlick had no clue and limited connections he used Japes to bring in a new Director of Sales. Over the years, Japes kept in touch with his old pal Sot from the Land of Empires. Sot, as proved inevitable with all Harsh' executives, was fired and searching for a new gig. He and Bootlick hit it off quite well and a new era of reckless abandonment would descend upon the hotel. Unfortunately, although the humor and gaiety abounded, the waters did become a bit muddied with this characters lack of ethics and morality. He commanded two exceptional skills, he sold hotel rooms with the best of them, and he hired the prettiest girls the sales office would ever see. When the economy hit a slump, it behooved the hotel to solicit discounted base business. Sot and his team filled that need and so began the climb to profitability. He told Japes that he would hire only the best looking and in his opinion the most qualified sellers. One could only imagine what his qualifications were. He indeed hired his administrator for the simple fact that she lived in his hometown and could at times give him a ride to work. It did not hurt that she was attractive and ignored his obvious shenanigans. The remainder of the sales staff', were all knockout blondes eager to please. To their credit they each were excellent at selling and would achieve success long after Sot left the property.

To this point, Japes could not understand what kept Sot and him connected. It certainly was not their integrity or morality, as they were at the opposite ends of the spectrum. Sot understood people, and in large part this skill propelled him through a successful career. He knew people well and during this period endeared himself to Japes forever. Invited to Sot's home one late fall day to watch an important football game, Japes grinned from ear to ear. The entire family, covered with their beloved team's blue and white logo from head to toe, huddled around the television. His High-fall Bills were knocking on the playoff door and needed only one more victory. An attractive tall brunette woman, appearing to be there on her own, sat to the side. Sot and his wife had played matchmaker and Jules would eventually become Japes wife. The two hit it off and by luck or by skill Sot provided this grand gesture of love. Jules, to this day, claims it was Sot's wife but no one will ever know.

Everyone enjoyed having fun at this time, as a greater emphasis had been placed on the happiness of the employees than that of the guests. A significant variation from the typical dictatorial hierarchy normally set forth in the archaic hotel cultures. The archaic philosophy, that the guest is always right, never sat well with Japes. For the most part, this new way of doing things proved effective as servers have this incessant need to please everyone and to be happy. Sot, however, saw this as an opportunity to play games and to fulfill his hedonistic and maniacal self-defacing desires. His hometown football team the High-fall Bills, for the first time in their history, were going to the Super Bowl. Japes managed to finagle two tickets through his connections, and as a lifelong fan of the Empire Giants thought he and Sot would have some fun. When arriving at the stadium, ten hours before game time, Sot connected with a bevy of his High-fall mongrel cohorts. After a dozen beers and a couple of sausages it became apparent that Japes would need to lock the tickets in the trunk of his car. Sot's friends drove a thousand miles without tickets. Not a smart move for the High-fall crowd, as the tickets were being scalped for $2,000 a pop. The outcome of the game showed a historical victory for the Giants, and Japes declared it to be the last Super Bowl he would venture to with Sot and his friends.

It just so happened by some miracle the Bills made it to the Super Bowl again the next year. Sot hounded Japes for tickets, which Japes had purchased through his uncles corporate offices. Japes refused as he knew darn well Sot experienced plenty of fun in his life, and perhaps he tipped the scales a little too far in his own direction. Unbeknownst to Japes, Sot rifled through his address book, telephoned his uncle's company, and impersonated Japes while speaking to the administrator from whom the tickets were obtained the prior year. Sot connived to get four tickets to the game and packaged such a deal whereby he actually made money on the trip. One early Monday morning Japes received a phone call from his irate uncle. He had been embarrassed at an executive board meeting by one of his counterparts. "UJ we would be able to address those issues if we weren't so busy rustling up Super Bowl tickets for your nephew" stated the stadium president. UJ had no idea what his counterpart was talking about. Japes apologized profusely, and after a lengthy interrogation and many cocktails he plied the truth out of Sot. This exposed a new low, even for the knucklehead from High-falls.

The housekeeping department had been running below standard for some time. Applying enough pressure to make improvements over the prior two years caused the housekeeper, Pillows, to look for a new position. It seemed funny to Japes that whenever she wore sneakers she worked diligently and inspected guest rooms. The problem, Pillows did not wear sneakers often enough, and in fact she usually wore immaculate dress shoes. The old saying you can expect what you inspect will forever be true in the area of cleanliness. A middle-aged server with graying hair who held a passionate love for her grandchildren, She appeared, for the most part, either disheveled or preoccupied when Japes approached her as he moved around the hotel. Pillows, on the other hand, made a wonderful presentation and looked like a million bucks when she would come into Jape's office for a meeting, another common theme of middle management using the Kiva tactic to stay in good graces with the decision-makers. The hotel world is one for behaviorists with the ability to evaluate in an instant whether it be, a customer, an employee, a manager, a vendor, and of course the boss.

The new kid on the block would fulfill one hundred percent of the standards and would stay at the facility for more than a decade. All the accomplished servers were usually found through networking with trusted friends as opposed to recruitment through headhunters. Obviously, one has to have the skills to evaluate in an interview and if possible an informal group meeting requiring interaction with others. Bootlick's infamous question to all candidates asked simply "If you could be any animal other than a human what would you be and why?" He would ask. The answer had no bearing whatsoever on a candidates future behavior or skill level, but it made him feel special as though he possessed some secret fantasmical power like superman. Despite this embarrassing show, Japes hired an executive housekeeper referred to him by Sot named Throwback. Throwback, a young Red-faced server, dressed immaculately, actively listened, looked Irish through and through, and was a doer. "Manager of the year" at a competitive hotel, his work ethic appeared beyond reproach. Throwback reminded Japes in a philosophical manner of the older employees within the hotel world. He would nurture his staff, all from a far away land, and extend himself to make everyone comfortable and happy in their roles. Throwback, not only a doer in the sense of getting the job done, but a doer in chasing skirts, whereby he utilized the employee rate offering at every hotel within a thirty-mile radius on every day of the week during his early years. He also could drink with the best of them, as would be documented in a number of escapades. Referring Throwback turned out good, one of the rare good deeds performed by Sot. Maybe he felt bad about invading Japes privacy and embarrassing UJ in his board meeting, but more likely he just got lucky.

A once in a lifetime event occurred when Japes and Jules tied the knot and the celebration was attended entirely by servers. Everyone either worked in a hotel or was a natural born server. All-in and his wife Liz had just moved across the country from the midland region. Mac and Hot-hips took a rare day off from boating. Elko, Capes, and many more from the Harsh Hotels all reconnected at the soiree. It felt like old home days. Sot imbibed to his heart's content and took full credit for the nuptials. There were nearly one hundred servers gathered in a small estate far off the beaten path. While the proud father, Jerry, sang "Neil Diamond" throughout the evening many gifted dancers cut the rug in what normally represented the library. A rare occasion when the servers were served, allowed everyone to cut loose and nobody spent a dime. The party offered, open everything, including guest rooms and rides home at nights end. It reminded Japes of the "old days" when his parents would host cocktail parties at their resort. Not many of the world's problems were solved that night, but most were discussed. The night proved a great success not only for the celebration, but the pure joy of being surrounded by happy servers. At evenings end Japes and his brother in law approached the weary bartender. Since the soiree offered an open bar everyone tipped incessantly to the point where he made over one thousand dollars. Upon request, he informed the boys that every drop of alcohol had been consumed except for this one remaining bottle of vodka. "I'll take it," declared Dan and he gave him forty bucks. This punctuated the perfect ending with a late night toast for the few still standing.

THE EARLY YEARS

Generally speaking, the core group that would run the hotel was assembled, though over the years there would be a few key additions to this team of hoteliers. Hotels, for the most part, are no different than living in a big home with a throng of activities. No two days are the same, especially when there are between two hundred and four hundred guests coming and going, and one hundred servers scattered throughout to service each other. The beauty of it comes not only from the satisfaction of helping others, but from the wonderful stories and situations that abound nowhere else on the planet. Typically a hotel would conduct a weekly staff meeting to review upcoming business, ongoing projects, and provide an open forum for each server to vent. Expressing felt good for all, as everyone needed to sing their own song. The Oasis maintained an open forum and encouraged communication at every level and as long as Bootlick remained 'out of the loop' there would be no shortage of stories.

A nasty situation occurred one summer when everyone noticed that a multitude of common houseflies were gaining entry into the hotel by way of the loading dock door. The early-morning servers would hose down the loading dock area and make certain the dumpster was closed tight. Adjacent to the dumpster were two fifty gallon drums full of grease that stunk to high heaven, but were necessary as the grease was removed and recycled on a weekly basis. This major calamity became quite the topic at staff and sanitation meetings throughout the hotel. Ho-hum, suggested the hotel purchase an air wall which, when the back door opened, would blow air straight down thus making it impossible for the flies to get in. Everyone felt the cost of the air curtain seemed prohibitive for such an obvious problem, the proposal eventually died in committee Oftentimes the back door remained propped open as to let some air flow to the back hall allowing the workers to stay cool. Bouncy, one of the dish dogs, asked if he could have a screen door placed in the back, thus keeping out the flies and keeping the workers cool. For security reasons, this would never happen. The situation had been analyzed to death for three weeks with no resolution at hand. Japes thought if the discussion lasted long enough, it would become autumn and the flies would be gone. Finally, at the end of one staff meeting when most had left, Elko came to an epiphany he had the solution. He suggested that the hotel purchase a dozen bat's with their houses. They would be strategically placed around the rear of the building. At night, along with the great white owl who sat perched on the enormous dogwood next to the dumpster, these creatures of the night would devour both the rodents and the flies. Japes, curious as to how the guests sitting on their patios would react to bat's whistling by their heads, noted that bats eat mosquitos not flies. The remaining servers at the meeting were laughing so hard they started to cry. What a creative solution this would have been. In the end, Waldo went out to the loading dock and hung five fly strips on the ceiling. He caught the majority of the flies and disposed of them each week.

Early one December evening the hotel bustled with activity stemming from the holiday parties, when the weather turned ugly forecasting ten to twelve inches of new snow. Most of the management team remained on the property that evening attending to various parties and normal responsibilities. Suddenly Dora, the restaurant manager, came running to the desk shouting there was an emergency in the restaurant. Dora, a young, naïve, wide-eyed server who walked like a duck rarely became animated. An excellent server who over time would become one of the best junior managers the hotel employed. She remained level headed at all times, therefore her yelling for help signaled something quite amiss. Japes approached the fine dining restaurant to see a number of managers, including Throwback, Ho-hum, and others kneeling beside a female guest lying on the floor. The staff had telephoned 911 and anxiously awaited emergency medical help. With the terrible weather outside everyone felt uncertain as to how long it would take. Much to everyone's dismay, the women delivered a baby right in the middle of the restaurant. Even the UPS driver, uncharacteristically in a panic, stood by to do whatever he could. The baby delivered just as the paramedics arrived at the front door, were escorted directly into the restaurant. There is no way on the face of the earth this woman should have been eating and drinking in a restaurant when she was about to deliver a baby. The staff and paramedics both knew something seemed amiss and it would be weeks before the truth would come out. The management team had done a fantastic job and delivered a child. Ho-hum's only concern encompassed being able to clean the carpet in his dining room so as not to inconvenience any of his patrons. Despite that, everyone looked truly amazed with the spectacular event. Throwback, who maintained contacts with the hospital, learned that the mother traveled under a false name, was full of barbiturates during the birthing, and was unable to pay for her room. The loss of the baby's life had been the saddest and by far the most tragic part of the story. People just do things in hotels that you couldn't possibly imagine.

The hotel held its annual Christmas celebration for all the servers in the month of January. The holiday season kept the entire staff extremely busy while servicing all the various parties being held in December. Japes and the executives decided to do trades with local businesses in exchange for an off-site party. The first Christmas party they

164

held in this manner took place at a restaurant called Wee-Wee's directly across the street. The restaurant offered a fantastic venue with plenty of seating, a nice bar, and excellent cuisine for all. In exchange, Wee-Wee's, would have their holiday party back at the hotel the following week. Japes handed out tickets for drinks to all the servers who attended. He gave out handfuls of tickets and none went to waste. Every server who attended the party drank to his or her heart's content. There were a great number servers' pickled to the n'th degree. After the employee of the year received an award for her contributions to the hotel, the crowd started to thin out, and the after party commenced. Elko appeared most excited after being hit on by Slinky one of the sexy sales servers. The same held true with Throwback and a number of the other managers. Needless to say a fair number of secret rendezvous occurred that evening, and few, if any could remember their partner. Bootlick hammered out of his tree, decided to drive home, but the local cops stopped him as his car weaved out of the parking lot. Lucky for him, the cop had a sense of humor and laughed at his musical Christmas socks. By pure luck, the fearless leader escaped, but of course, the cop seen regularly for the next year eating a free brunch and occasionally spending the night, cashed in his reward.

One of the boldest moves that Japes pulled off during his tenure at the Hotel involved the rehiring of Casanova upon his release from prison. The day after leaving Casanova showed up to ask for his job back. Japes explained that the front office management position was taken, but that he would keep his word and carve a way for him to become the supreme commander of the overnight shift. Casanova would be taken care of despite the threats made by the HR department and Scam himself. These two entities would never think of sticking their necks out for a fellow server in need. Japes did not care what they said as they both were the epitome of a succubus. Casanova, however, didn't always make it easy for Japes to keep him under the radar. His conquests became the topic of discussion within the subculture known as " the night shift" which eventually made it to the day shift. He proudly boasted of conquering one beautiful German girl inside the gift shop. This area would be more appropriately named "The lift shop" in the years ahead. The episode that brought his behavior to light occurred when Mr. Casanova found the urge to make a little whoopee in Japes office. The office desk constructed with a large laminated structure had been in the office since the hotel opened. Upon arrival one morning, Japes noticed the middle of his desk appeared to have a distinct bow in it. Casanova admitted years later, after repeated questioning, that he had had his way with a server on his desk. He said, with a robust grin on his face, "I had an itch that needed scratching! Do you know what I mean, ha ha ha," Japes didn't know what he meant, and asked him to refrain from any and all such urges at the hotel! There was only so much a server could do for someone a little discretion would go a long way.

Both the front office and sales office would turn over on average every two years. The front office management represented a hotspot as hundreds of thousands of guests registered each year. It was challenging to take care of these duties and not become stressed. Likewise, coordinating and maintaining the large number of groups and preferred customers, to meet the financial goals of the business, required true skill. The youngest and the best front office manager that worked for Japes, Casper, earned a promotion to a supervisor's position during these early years. Demonstrating exceptional skills with the customer and organizing the desk lifted the department to a new level. Japes promoted Casper to front office manager, as the service scores were the highest they had ever been. Japes took him under his wing and coached him as best he could on how to manage the staff. Casper looked like a life size Pillsbury Dough Boy and epitomized a server who wanted to please. Japes, taking from his past, played a few rounds of golf with Casper and they built a good relationship. In a short time Casper built a strong team and would be recognized by the company as their future. One story goes as he went to the movies with a girl named Cheryl she put her hand on his tally-whacker and started to squeeze. He became so upset that he took the girl home and told the gang that he had never been so horrified in his entire life. His fear of women, however, did seem a little peculiar to both Throwback, who he hung out with, and Japes. At the time, everyone just laughed at him as they thought he portrayed a scared virgin.

The operational servers viewed the sales department a differently than others. All the operational server saw were well groomed and well dressed servers sitting in an office from nine to five, never on the weekends, never during strange hours, and never sweating. They possessed a different skill set from the majority of servers scattered throughout the hotel, and they were seen as free game. Roach, one of the desk supervisors, a young French server who spoke with a heavy accent and enjoyed quite the reputation as a ladies man, prowled the flock. Not particularly good-looking, with a long crooked nose, eyebrows straight across, and weighing in at hundred and forty pounds soaking wet, he ambitiously pursued a number of the sales servers and predominantly secured an emphatic shut down. Slinky, a seasoned veteran of the sales world earned her nickname from her beautiful stride as she walked by. She did not walk; she slid across the floor as her physique moved in a perfect rhythm for the boys to admire. Her posterior would be classified a ten out of ten on the callipygous scale. Although Roach pursued Slinky with the zeal of a bee searching for nectar his advances proved unsuccessful. He did, however, make headway with a twenty two-year-old blonde bombshell named Tena. Roach's demise came just one month after hooking up with the bombshell. He bragged amongst his peers of his conquest, and the young lady's great ability in the boudoir. The young girl, feeling betrayed and humiliated dropped a dime on the server to the corporate offices informing them that he used hotel funds from his bank for personal reasons. Japes, forced to audit his bank, discovered that there were hundreds of dollars missing. When confronted Roach admitted he borrowed money from his bank to pay for dates with Tena. A direct violation of all policies the poor server was forced to find another job, and maybe, just maybe, he would learn to keep his mouth shut.

The highlight of the early years culminated with a distinguished award called The Superior Hotel Award. This recognition, presented to one hundred hotels throughout the system, which included four thousand hotels worldwide, surprised everyone. The award recognized not only the outstanding service provided by the staff, but also the cleanliness of the hotel and the fine appointment of the facility. The prominent players on the management staff who made this possible included Throwback and Casper. Their courteous and efficient staffs provided excellent feedback with positive comments from all the customers who stayed both in the corporate and leisure markets. In fact Shuffle-head, the franchise inspector', so impressed by the guest room maids who sang as they performed their daily duties claimed this action alone was the tipping point that put them over the top. The beautiful trophy prominently displayed in the lobby for all to see brought smiles to all. The owners were happy with the growing success of the business as they received more and more positive comments along with increased profits. Japes honest system, albeit rarely used, resulted in success. The group's cohesion, increased as the result of attaining this common non-financial goal. Scam, at this time, curious as to what Japes would like to do in the future, made inquiries. He informed Scam that he would like to be the general manager of the hotel as he felt this a perfect fit for his skills and experience. Who knew what would happen in the future, but that would be the only position Japes would be interested in within the company. For true success every aspect of a leaders' engagement with an organization must be on an equal footing. This includes both personal and professional honesty.

It ended in a toss up between Waldo and Sot as to who carried on the most destructive lifestyle. Waldo, a bit of a mystery to everyone, although remaining in everyones good graces, he was not well respected and the saying "Where's Waldo" befitted him. The little round server looked as if he was going to split a button as his shirt and pants fitted tightly around his round belly. More and more frequently it became impossible to find him when something needed to be done. He would always agree with Japes with whatever duty asked of him, but for some reason whatever they agreed upon he would never do. He fell into a relationship with one of the supervisors in the hotel named Silly. The grapevine concluded that Waldo and Silly were spending "quality time" testing the beds in the hotel and often planning a secret rendezvous outside the property. Waldo married with two young children, and although, nobody on the staff approved of his exploits they certainly would never drop a dime on him. Toy and Big Apple were relentless with their harassment of Waldo, not only did they embarrass him publicly, behind-the-scenes they portrayed him as a cheater. Japes knew the end grew near for Waldo when he called out sick one day, stating for the second time that his mom had passed away. Japes, albeit a compassionate server felt quite certain that his mother could only die once. So happened that Silly, during the same period, traveled on vacation to the desert. When Waldo finally returned to work he had a deep suntan, which Japes thought unusual considering his family lived in the Land of Empires and the weather had been inclement over the past week. This event marked the last time that Waldo would lie to Japes.

Sot stood not far behind in his debauchery and just plain stupidity as an executive in the hotel. Some of his antics included getting so inebriated during a New Year's Eve celebration that he was forced to spend the evening at the hotel. Found on the top floor wandering around peeing in a planter by the elevator landing, raised a few eyebrows. Evidently, he lost the key to his room and stumbled about looking for another drink. This accompanied the usual rumors, including his shagging of a hot desk clerk name Poison Ivy. A young server with bedroom eyes aimed at any man in a suit. An unwed mother of two forced to relinquish the custody of her own children, characterizing the last woman on the face of the earth that Sot or anybody else should be involved with. He was not that selective, and if it involved drinking to excess, well then, Sot perched at the forefront of his profession.

Japes, Bootlick, and Sot went on a road trip for dinner and drinks to celebrate the upcoming nuptials for Bootlick. After a few hours of heavy libations followed by heavier libations the three headed home with Japes behind the wheel driving Sot's car. Sot hammered so out of his mind that while going seventy miles an hour he pulled on the emergency brake nearly killing them all. Japes, fortunately, managed to finagle Bootlick back home and proceed to schlep Sot to his home for the evening. At three in the morning, Japes awoke to the sound of Sot driving his car away and leaving Japes with no transportation to work the next day. Sot knew his wife would kill him if he didn't come home and Japes could fend for himself. Japes never learned his lesson after all those years.

Finally, after many years of fumbling around with incompetent maintenance men Japes hired Chief. Chief was a Midland server the looked more like an executive or even an owner than he did a maintenance man. Fantastic when running the morning lobby lizard program whereby each manager on a given day would greet all incoming and outgoing guests, Japes would often be asked if that gentleman owned the hotel. On his first official day Chief was hustled onto a bus with the entire management staff to participate in a Halloween trip to the North Shore. The group started drinking at noon and Chief, thank Mother Nature, was not scared off by such crazy behavior. He had been a rope burner in his day and after sewing his oats during the 60's and early 70's he gravitated to the hotel world. He thought it better to make a living managing a staff instead of pounding nails. Experienced with all the trades as a result of working a little in all of them, he exemplified the proverbial "jack of all trades." He would fight his own battles, survive the inevitable change of executives, and eventually even the change in ownership. Of all the servers Chief would garner the longest tenure and the greatest stamina.

Scam, nicknamed Little Caesar by Vick the van driver, without a doubt, symbolized the most appropriate description for the homuncule that any server could have come up with.

Well, in his infinite wisdom, Scam promoted Sot from Director of Sales at the hotel to a regional sales manager overseeing five different properties. Apparently, Sot's drunken escapades provided the sound foundation needed for such a promotion. Scam wanted another puppet that he could control, but would soon discover that this decision along with the majority of his decisions proved a mistake. As a businessman, Scam held a position of power and everybody knew it. As a purveyor of alternate truths he had no peers. The hotel servers continued to feel secure knowing that Little Caesar stood less informed than Bootlick and their culture would remain intact. Who in their right mind would promote a server who could not even control his own life? The writing was on the wall for the calamity stricken Sot, but over the next few months he would be certain to leave a lasting impression with the company. Besides padding his expense reports by coding strip club expenses as meals with clients, Sot discovered new ways to screw up. During a trip to the Lowlands with one of his subordinates, Sot and the sales manager became thoroughly hammered at a club. Upon returning to their hotel, the two were stopped and the subordinate arrested for driving under the influence. In a panic, fearing for his job, Sot telephoned Japes and asked for two thousand dollars to post bail so that his subordinate could get out of jail and fly home. Sot wanted to keep everything under the radar so both his boss and his wife would never find out. Japes finally came to his senses and told him not only would he not give him any money, but he and he alone was responsible for the subordinate during the trip and the company as a whole could be liable. He was on his own and somehow managed to keep the truth from ever coming out.

Sot would often call the hotel at wee hours of the night and speak to Casanova. A typical night would involve Casanova talking constantly to Sot so he would stay awake while driving to his home. He would give him various landmarks so Casanova could figure out which highway or back road Sot traveled on. He would then direct him home and keep him awake so he did not pass out and kill himself or someone else. The straw that broke the camels back involved the extravaganza Sot and Bootlick planned for Sot's wife's fortieth birthday party. He invited many of the hotel executives, sales managers, and friends of the company to a soirée at the Oasis. The entire event, subsidized by the hotel with Scam being the only prominent server not in attendance proved a fatal error. Upon learning about this abuse of authority and not being invited to the party the dwarf became enraged. Apparently, Sot's jokes about Scam's feet never hitting the floor from his seat on the plane and other assorted wisecracks along with this final event proved all that Scam could take. Bootlick, although he approved all these expenses, slid by without a scratch. This calamity finalized the tragic end for one fun loving server.

Casper, the crown jewel of the hotel, could do no wrong, he grew into such a nice server that he even dressed up like a clown for one of the manager's children's birthday party. The guests and the staff at the desk loved him as he took care of their needs. A few days after one of the infamous Christmas parties Japes spoke with a local detective. The holiday party was a typical drinking Fest which included Bootlick sliding across the dance floor imitating Elvis, and the employee of the year being so cocked he could not even speak. Japes felt certain that the police officer appeared as a result of inappropriate behavior by a partygoer. The police informed Japes that a complaint surfaced concerning Casper and one of the bellmen. Apparently, according the young bellmen, Casper and he shared a room at the hotel after the Christmas party. He claimed that Casper exposed himself that evening. After investigating the police found evidence that Casper had been in a scuffle with yet another one of the young bellmen. Japes wondered why Casper had a black eye and it was revealed that the bellman's brother punched him in the face. Despite this, Japes, indignant to the accusations, asked the police to leave the property. Unless they produced actual facts corroborating "the story" and intended to arrest Casper of a crime he would not accuse him. On the other hand,

Bootlick, did not want anything to do with even the appearance of improper conduct and the publicity it would cause. He would not defend Casper and fight for his job and reputation despite his great contributions to the hotel. Casper was instead fired for staying overnight on the property without the approval of management as none of the accusations concerning the bellmen could be proved. With tears flowing, Japes made the announcement that Casper would no longer be working at the Oasis and cited only the unauthorized use of a guest room as the reason. The hypocrisy of Bootlick and Scam reached beyond belief, as a week had not gone by when they skirted any number of company policies. By far the saddest day at the Oasis rocked the gang to their core.

Tasmania, a young supervisor that took over for Casper, commanded a high-energy level, maintained a great physical condition, and kept totally motivated at all times. He worked fast and expected everyone to keep pace with him. Although there was some turnover as a result of Casper leaving Tasmania kept the office running at a high level. He understood all that transpired with Casper and remained well versed in what to communicate, making sure that no important decisions ever hit Bootlick's desk. He would thrive in the culture and learn many new skills in a short period of time. Eventually, Tasmania, moved on and became a successful general manager in his own right.   Unique situations became prevalent during this period for no apparent reason. A tall, slender server in his late twenties named Creepy worked on the maintenance team, and although a little peculiar seemed to fit in well. He even came up with some novel ideas such as putting in turnstiles and charging each guest a quarter to use the pool facilities. One evening, after a hard day's work, Japes and other staff members were shocked to see Creepy on the local news as the lead story. An undercover investigation concerning Creepy, allegedly luring teenagers back to his home hit the six o'clock news. He acted like the last person anyone would have imagined could do such a thing. Eventually culminating with a plea bargain, Creepy left for a stint in "The Big House." Years later, on Spank-vision, a hotel staff member pointed out an unbelievable pornographic show. The show entitled, "The Houston One Hundred", involved a number of men participating in an orgy. Midway through the film, low and behold Creepy engaged with the lead character. It is rumored to this day that Creepy had become the king of hotel porn.

Hard to believe that it could happen in this affluent area, but it seemed as though the hotel was besieged with a rash of deviant behavior. One afternoon a reservation server went to the ladies room in the main lobby. The ladies' room looked elegant and in fact many that were in the area shopping or doing business would oftentimes stop in just to use the facility. The reservation server came running out of the ladies room screaming at the front desk that she had been violated. Upon calming down, she explained a man slid under the door flat on his back and looked up her skirt while she sat on the commode. The perverse man giggled and said everything looks fine slid out and ran away. All the servers from the management staff scurried about the hotel, and a few ran across four lanes of highway trying to catch this bizarre character. Even the police with an artist sketch were unable to catch this backsliding peeper.

At the same time, the hotel initiated the process of performing what is known in the hotel industry as a PIP. A PIP represents the product improvement plan, which is required by the franchise and most financial institutions. Each phase of the project would cost hundreds of thousands of dollars and required a large number of vendors. Elko took responsibility for obtaining and evaluating all the various bids with a common scope of work for each. Elko, became entrenched in the culture and even hosted parties at his beachside home for the staff. Not beyond reproach, and obtaining a number of favors from many vendors, his office was scattered with mirrors displaying various brands of beer, and other such giveaways. The free load of sifted loam delivered to his home from the approved landscape vendor, perhaps represented the most outrageous skirting of the rules that Elko engaged in. After presenting the bids for the first phase of the renovations Japes, Elko, and Bootlick all noticed that Scam approved a vendor not even on the list. It also seemed strange that this particular vendor bid exactly ten dollars less than his rival. Even stranger, once the project started, the entire scope of work changed from the original plans. The not surprising development was that the vendor turned out to be a friend of Scam's, and the two would take from the owners on every project they could. When all of these facts were presented at a staff meeting, Scam simply glared across the boardroom table at Elko and stated, "If you want to wrestle with me you're going to lose". Bootlick, within two months, eliminated the purchasing position and Elko lost his job.

During his last days Elko remained positive and did not lose his unique sense of humor. The staff would often times hold their weekly meeting on the top floor of the hotel. From the lounge, everyone could view the main street and the surrounding malls. At this last meeting with Elko, the staff noticed a man standing out front with a sign wrapped around his neck. A homeless man frequently stood in front of the hotel with a sign stating, "Will work for food". This time, however, it was not a homeless man it was Elko with a huge smile on his face. He showed a lot of class for someone who received a raw deal. The tip of the iceberg when it came to Scam and Bootlick.

THE GLORY YEARS

The group, resilient enough to withstand these harsh blows to their family, forged ahead. It brought everyone closer and even more committed to each other, with the realization, at least in Japes mind, that Bootlick had no integrity and that Scam acted like an old-fashioned taker who would do anything to keep his position. The group's cohesion, increased with the recognition of a common adversary. Despite these setbacks, the hotel remained in the middle of a service and financial windfall that would last for years. The customers became so familiar with the hotel servers that many were on a first name basis. The Keebler lady, a wonderful middle-aged patron who worked as a sales executive, would often times bring cookies for everybody that she saw. She would contribute to various hotel charities and even one year participated in Big Apple's football pool. She shared in the joy of hotel staff weddings, newborns, and other important life events. Likewise, Japes, always made certain the Keebler lady received a room no matter how busy, as she represented one of the many regular customers who spread the good word and helped nurture this tremendous success.

Because of the hotel's reputation a number of new opportunities arose. One such booking included a visit by the current Ms. America. A stunning beauty named Pinto with a Polynesian background and a smile that just wouldn't quit graced the community. Sponsored by a national cosmetic company, Pinto held a press conference in one of the private meeting rooms turning everyones head she necessitated a hotel-wide code blue. This term affectionately used by the male staff whenever a beautiful woman entered the premises, commanded attention. The walkie-talkies were left on at all times by key personnel to sound the alert. Miss America had been booked into the presidential suite for the one night and retired rather early after dinner. The suite was essentially one large room with a row of bookcases in the middle dividing the sitting area and the sleeping room. The next morning in the main lobby, after getting a real nice smooch, Japes wished the beautiful woman a pleasant day as she went on her way. He noticed that Throwback and a couple of the supervisors were snickering in the corner of the lobby and started laughing out loud as she left. "What the hell's going on guys?" asked Japes. "Well, you got a nice smooch boss, but let me tell you something if you saw the whole picture you would have popped your screws right then and there" laughed Throwback. "What do you mean?" Asked Japes. "We took it upon ourselves to reverse the peephole in the door entering the suite. The show last night, although only for a second as her bodyguard stayed directly across the hall, when Miss America decided to retire was fantastic, and we all strongly believe she is the most beautiful girl in

182

the world. " Truth was they did not see anything, but the escapade itself lifted morale to an all-time high.

Perhaps the funniest interlude ever experienced by Throwback was told to Japes in the cafeteria one day. Part of Throwbacks duties included inspecting rooms to make sure they were properly cleaned and often times simply to double check and make sure that the guests checked out. The hotel was so busy that they sold out every Monday through Thursday year-round. Throwback knocked on a door of what was known as a discrepant room, which meant the desk did not know if it remained occupied or vacant. After repeatedly knocking on the door, he opened to see a young, vibrant couple having sex in positions that even embarrassed him. He immediately closed the door and went back to tell the front office that the room remained occupied. The desk informed Throwback that the room had been rented and that the couple must check out. He would go back in a few hours to inform the couple. After time elapsed, he again knocked repeatedly on the door, but to no avail. Upon entering the room for the second time he again observed the ultimate in frolicking by the couple. This time, however, he kept waving his hands and yelling to gain the attention of one of the guests. Finally, the woman jumped out of bed and immediately covered herself. At that moment, Throwback realized that both the patrons were deaf. They had no idea he had entered the room or that they needed to check out. During the entire interlude Throwback thought they were so enthralled with their lovemaking that they simply ignored him.

Every spring the hotel accommodated an unusual group. An organization that evaluated young artists for a career in the performing arts overtook the hotel. Primarily, they evaluated young and upcoming actors, but they also observed singing and dancing. Teenagers would come from all over the country to meet various producers, directors, and choreographers who held private auditions for the opportunity to make it in theater or even in Hollywood. The hotel, much to the maintenance department's chagrin, would be required to remove all furniture from every room on the first floor as these rooms were used for the auditions. A wonderful piece of business during a slow time of year, allowing the hotel to sell every guest room for a span of four days and provide hundreds of lunches to all the participants. Upon entering one of the audition rooms Throwback and Silly were taken by surprise. Seeing this beautiful young lady, with her head firmly entrenched in the lap of a director, enraged them both. Apparently, these directors and producers were living up to their reputations of being complete dirt bags. Over the years, the staff learned that this common practice affected more than anyone could have imagined. The entire industry, referred to by the operation servers as the "Empire of Sleaze", gave everyone the creeps, and they cautioned all the young applicants to its pitfalls.

Bezzel, one of the housemen who worked for Pepe' Le Fete in the banquet department, was a small server from the subcontinent who always had a smile on his face and loved everybody. A hard worker, both he and his brother came from different careers. In their home country, he drove a truck and his brother practiced the law. Immigrating to this country and searching for work encompassed their lives, offering them an opportunity to provide for their families. Although hard to communicate due to the language barrier, it appeared evident to Japes and all the managers that these two servers purported a different agenda than most. Always winking and smiling at each other as if they were the masterminds, of some worldwide scheme filled their days. While a number of managers and employees were at an employee of the month luncheon, the front office interrupted and asked Japes to come to the front desk. Japes, upon arriving at the desk, greeted by a well-groomed FBI agent asking for a moment of his time, he showed Japes pictures of people entering and exiting a local bank. The agent asked if he recognized the individual in the photograph. Japes told the agent that he had no idea who it was, but if he left the picture he would check with the managers. The agent expounded that this person, cashing $20,000 checks every week, participated in a cash laundering enterprise that extended from the Flatlands to Cod City. Upon returning to the luncheon, Japes and the gang realized that it looked a lot like Bezzel's brother, Emm, who cashed the checks, but they weren't quite sure. It never mattered, as Bezzell and his brother did not show up for work that day, and were never seen again by anyone.

The cafeteria, without a doubt, offered much more than a place to eat lunch or dinner. The inner sanctum of the hotel where, over the decades, more managing and problem solving transpired than in any office or formalized meeting. A proverbial melting pot of line staff and management encompassing many different languages and a myriad of mores, welcomed the masses. Over the years, most of the vendors would work their schedules so they could stop in and have lunch with the gang Monday through Friday at 12:30 PM. The sales girls, referred to as the lunch bunch, insisted on healthy foods, including a pristine salad bar and whole grain breads while the guys' yearned for meat and potato. It was nothing for the chef to occasionally deep fry a turkey or serve lobster bisque as a treat. A typical lunch conversation involved a lot of laughter, a lot of head shaking, and most importantly a continuum of bonding between servers.

Capes' assistant, Sodumb, down in the dumps one day, decided to sit with the guys and complain about her husband. She told everybody that he was a lazy slug; he sat around the house in his underwear eating fried chicken and watching stupid sports on TV all day. All she wanted him to do was mow the lawn. After about twenty minutes of complaining the guys told Sodumb that any one of them would be happy to mow her lawn. They repeated it a number of times as to how much enjoyment they would receive in mowing her lawn and make sure she was happy. At the end of the lunch, she thanked the guys for listening and looked happy that someone could empathize with her predicament. Apparently, unfamiliar with the connotation of "mow your lawn" the remaining gang simultaneously shook their heads and smiled. The encounter erupted into a gut buster for the boys and an eye-opener for Japes as to Sodumb's naivety.

As funny as that situation played out, Pepe' Le Fete, perpetrated the funniest outburst in the cafeteria. Boo-boo, the banquet clown, who, although forty-five years old, for some reason decided he should be circumcised. Nobody could figure out who told him to do this and even his wife being a nurse you would think would tell him it was an unnecessary operation. The entire banquet staff had a strange habit of flipping their wrist horizontally and snapping their fingers. It looked almost like a backhanded slap, but a much quicker and a more violent action. Boo-boo, maybe five feet tall, returning to work a couple of days after his operation stood next to Pepe' Le Fete in the cafeteria incessantly complaining about some nonsensical mundane

187

task as he sat trying to eat. Pepe' Le Fete had had enough and in an instant with a quick flip of his wrist, he motioned for him to leave and inadvertently snapped Boo-Boo right at the end of his pecker. Boo-Boo doubled over and howled like a wolf crying in the night. It highlighted the last time he ever bothered Pepe' Le Fete at lunch.

The strangest couple to work at the hotel' were Moose and Mouse. Moose, although quite large, was a pleasant looking server who made a great presentation to customers and personified a happy front desk clerk. Mouse, on the other hand, portrayed a small server and performed many different jobs, including dishwashing, busing, and room service delivery during the slow periods. These two servers were known as the odd couple around the hotel as Moose looked at least double the size of Mouse. In their way each would cause great stress to the entire operation of the hotel. Moose, in her infinite wisdom, decided to give a guest room key to a person without checking for identification. In her defense, the perpetrator of this deception, well versed, took a perfect opportunity to confuse the young server. Unbeknownst to the hotel this imposter worked for a national television station and was investigating an undercover story about hotel security. The hotel owners unfortunately spent tens of thousands of dollars with a PR firm to prepare Bootlick for a live television interview, all in a hope to mitigate the terrible publicity. Japes defended Moose and in the end she kept her job. Mouse, on the other hand, would not be so lucky.

One day a beautiful middle-aged woman, approached Ho-hum and Japes in the lobby of the hotel. This lady described a story about a young server who knocked on her door with a room service order. After delivering the order, this little server admired the woman's hair and told her that he worked as a professional hairdresser and would be happy to give her a haircut. The woman declined the offer and became so uncomfortable that she insisted on speaking to management. Japes and Ho-hum were so dumbfounded by this revelation that they simply stared at the woman with open mouths shaking their heads in disbelief. Furthermore, she said the little server took it upon himself to visit her room two hours later and again solicit his hairdressing skills. Mouse was no hairdresser and in fact Japes and Ho-hum thought he truly lost his mind. It marked the last day Mouse would pretend to play hairdresser, as he went on his merry way with a strong recommendation to seek counseling.

Segue K, the hotel's concierge, was an elderly server who had the habit of carrying on at least four conversations within a two-minute period. She skipped around so much that even the greatest of listeners had trouble keeping up. Her best friend Madonna, the hotel's operator, was also an elderly server who became known as the voice of the hotel. The two were seen as the grandmothers to all the servers. At

189

lunch one day a rather delicate situation, at least in the minds of these ladies, was brought to Jape's attention. Evidently, an attractive young server named Foxy was reportedly strutting her stuff in the ladies locker room before and after taking a shower. Japes said to the ladies, "There is little I can do about a server flaunting their stuff. What would you like me to do?" Well, it's not so much she's strutting her stuff, but the fact that she is showering with other girls that is making us uncomfortable," Stated Segue K. It highlighted the only time in a decade that Segue K actually stayed on point when conversing with Japes. Nothing was ever said or done about the former stripper's bathroom routine as it turned out to be a one-time event.

The lunch bunch worked hard and attracted a number of unique groups to stay at the hotel. One of the regulars included a religious group that was often seen in neighborhoods expounding on their beliefs and trying to convert all who would listen to their religion. Another group the La leche League frequented the hotel every quarter. This league consisted of moms who would breast-feed their young until the child became disinterested no matter what the age. They could be seen throughout the hotel in various sitting areas some even exposed for everyone to see. The most interesting and by far the most unusual group, however, was the Fruit-fly group. The Fruit flies consisted mainly of male participants whose secret desire involved wearing women's underwear. They were not homosexuals, but for a treat they loved to dress up as women and be treated as such. The hotel, recommended because of its outstanding service and its ability to acquiesce to one and all, evolved into a gathering place. The only rule that the group insisted upon required that when they were seen as women they would be addressed as women. The truth of the matter was that this group paid more than any other group to use the facilities. Japes and the desk manager were standing out front when a large man named Fred approached the desk. The patron portrayed the spitting image of Fred Flintstone including the five o'clock shadow. He stated, "The next time you see me, I will not be recognizable, and my name will be Phyllis. I'm going to attend the fashion show being held in the ballroom," he/she stated. An hour later when Fred stopped by the desk again and everyone politely addressed her as Phyllis Japes nodded and she scurried on her way. It appeared completely insane as Fred looked like Fred wearing a dress with hairy arms, five o'clock shadow, and large enough to be the lineman on any football team.

In their infinite wisdom the sales team booked all three of these groups on the same weekend in the middle of February. Needless to say, the challenges were many and of particular interest was the designation of a gender-neutral bathroom. The Fruit flies felt it presented no problem for them to use the ladies room when they were in their dresses.

191

The actual ladies were shocked and dismayed at such a revelation. The Fruit flies also turned everyone's head in the pool, as they didn't exactly look like a girl in their bikinis. At one point, a fruit fly came to the desk and complained that a LaLeche woman exposed her breast in public and that "she" felt offended. Japes, leaned over, looked at the individual and said, "Are you kidding, this woman feeding her baby is the least of your concerns as we have fielded dozens of questions concerning your rather unusual group." "I see what you mean". Replied the fruiter. As he walked away one of the religious fanatics approached, and was heard trying to convert him to their way of thinking. It amounted to quite a circus, but all the groups made it through the weekend and no guests were any worse for the wear. As Mr. Smith, the group president, exited the hotel the following morning he looked back over his shoulder at Japes and stated, "Just remember every time you board an airplane one out of every twenty males is wearing women's underwear". The local chapter of this national group appreciated the atmosphere so much that they frequented the lobby bar every Thursday night dressed up in their best attire. Local and regular guests made it a point to stop in for a drink and see how the girls looked.

Trade outs became a large part of the culture when Bootlick took over as general manager. The hotel traded for more than just a Christmas party. The hotel traded with the local movie theater, the local liquor store, the local restaurants, a few vendors, and of course a car wash so Bootlick could have his car detailed. The hotel industry as a whole oftentimes did trades for overnight rooms all over the world. In fact, many of the hotel servers traveled in foreign lands, and throughout the continent at little or no cost. Every year Japes would work on a trade for the grand prize of a charity golf event benefiting the local hospital. The grand giveaway included airline tickets and a room for two at some exotic location. All of these trades benefited servers who worked at the hotel in one manner or another. This practice, encouraged by Bootlick and his boss simply because no expense would be shown on any financial statement, required merely a handshake and a nod between businesses.

During one lunch break the Chief, Throwback, and Japes were introduced to some outstanding chicken wings. When they learned that these wings came from a saloon called "The Chicken Bone" they were compelled to have a cocktail. This Thursday night tradition would continue for nearly twenty years. It became known as" Thirsty Thursday" and the three enjoyed cocktails and wings with virtually every manager who ever worked at the Oasis. Gilligan, one of the Bone's managers, would often time give Japes and Chief a free cocktail as they were big tippers and frequented the saloon on a consistent basis. The saloon stood as a watering hole for all the trades in the area and at one point or another every plumber, electrician, and carpenter exchanged drinks with the gang. The food tasted fantastic and the patrons would fight over a certain bar stool so they could observe the bartender's beautiful figures. The Bone became a gathering place once a week for the servers to highlight all the important gossip within the hotel and the company.

One of the most notorious visits to the hotel came from a builder who worked for the parent company that came to fill in the pool and construct a second ballroom. Conquer, a colorful character who stood about six foot three, and although he didn't wear a cowboy hat it would have been appropriate fired up the troops. Charged with the responsibility of filling in the pool and turning the large area into a unique ballroom all within a three-month timeframe seemed impossible. Yet, he pushed the local tradesmen to the limit and spent exorbitant amounts of money to meet the schedule. He and the Chief hit it off well and made a habit of reviewing the job with a few cocktails after work. Conquer loved his tequila. He saddled up to the bar at the Bone throwing down a one hundred dollar bill and asking them to keep bringing shots of tequila. Upon the first delivery, "You call that a shot" exclaimed Conquer. To satisfy him, the bartender from then on poured triple the normal amount in each glass. Occasionally, the Chief drove the entire way home with his head half out the window, not prone to vomiting it became a new and not so exciting experience for the seasoned veteran.

The entire plan to increase the meeting space originated with Capes, and Japes completed an extensive study to consider what would be lost in overnight room revenue. Capes's idea would be a home run for the hotel and increased revenues by nearly half a million dollars each year. He would never receive any credit for this great idea. It happened during the glory years of the hotel, but it also further enlightened the entire staff as to the true character of both Scam and Bootlick.

During this period a number of new servers found their way into the world. In the front office there was Smiles, a young, handsome college graduate who charmed the pants off of any girl he so desired. He made guests' happy and became a secret weapon when needing to deal with difficult situations. Smiles legendary charm included his rumored interlude with the Russian bombshell who hosted in the restaurant, the tabletop dance from the hottest maids, and of course the secret bachelor party held in the private concierge lounge featuring "the twins". He, however, remained discreet and by all observations a gentleman. Bubblehead, a server who had been recruited by Japes for many years, nurtured a reputation of a seasoned veteran who understood all the nuances of working at a four-star hotel. He made an exceptional presentation and along with

Smiles handled many of the difficult situations. The two became good buddies both in the hotel and in the outside world. They were two handsome chaps ready to set the world on fire, and on occasion load a little bump of white powder up their noses. To round out the dream team there was Oh. Oh, started working at the hotel as the pool boy at the ripe old age of seventeen. Gifted with a great personality and like most Irish servers he could consume large quantities of alcohol at a young age. He soon progressed to the front office and filled in all those gaps left by his coworkers. Highly intelligent and understanding the computer systems inside and out, he ran the show. If Smiles attitude couldn't take care of a problem, Oh would appeal to the intellect and bring the situation to a close. Oh could well have become a politician. A few situations defined his complexity showing the good the bad and the ugly of Oh. During a visit a customers' car had been broken into. The only items taken were a little patron's hockey equipment, as the family had come from far away for a tournament. Oh, totally empathetic with the customer, apologized profusely for the terrible incident and requested the police take all the information for insurance purposes. Thinking quickly and relying on his instincts Oh snuck home found his youth hockey equipment and brought it back to the hotel. He presented his youth equipment to the family and the young boy played in this important event. He embodied the true meaning of hospitality creatively displayed in a thoughtful manner.

Perhaps it stemmed from his age, but Oh, also had a dark side that developed over the years. Late one afternoon Japes received a telephone call from the front office stating that a customer had no credit and had not paid for his overnight room. The standard procedure required asking the customer for a new form of payment or credit would have to be established. The guest totally inebriated, but coherent enough to stagger to his room, refused to answer his telephone. Oh, finally, after being asked by Japes, meandered on up to the guest room and confronted the guest in-person. After refusing to establish credit, the heated discussion ended with Oh telling the guest that he had screwed his wife. This was not the "nuance of service' that Japes could have hoped for. Unfortunately, after getting a second call from the furious man, Japes, went to the guest room and discovered the out of control guest passed out on his bed. Ultimately, the customer had no money and had no intention of paying his bill. Japes let him sleep off the booze and he snuck out the next day. Oh, reprimanded for his lack of control, never looked back.

A few weeks later the corporate auditor visited the hotel to check out the controls. Oh, pointed out that there appeared to be a glitch in the credit card transmittal system, which allowed any agent to credit any credit card without it being offset. The auditor claimed this was impossible and not to be concerned with the balancing of the hotel. Subsequently, Oh would on occasion credit a co-workers credit card, including Japes, to see if the erroneous credit would be discovered. Japes, astonished that the credit went through and that the hotel appeared in balance, again, telephoned the corporate auditor, only to be told, " Do not be concerned". Nonetheless, Japes asked Oh to end this practice, and to this day it remains a real head scratcher.

Baby, the first true food and beverage director the hotel employed in many years, hailed from the Midland Region, always smiling with impeccable taste in her attire. She managed to put out the best special occasion banquets and unique events that the hotel had ever seen. Her Easter brunches were undoubtedly the best the area and perhaps even the city. The hotel purchased a life-size replica of Bugs Bunny and a number of other cartoon characters. There was even an exact replica of batman worn by one of the maintenance men. Children from miles away begged their parents to take them to the Easter brunch to see all the characters. It blossomed into an exceptional success not only for financial reasons, but also for public relations.

One year, Bobebbie, playing Bugs Bunny decided to take a break at her desk. The door to the main lobby remained propped open while she took her break, and decided to smoke a cigarette. When the little patrons observed a headless Bugs Bunny smoking a cigarette you would have thought the world had come to an end. Baby smoothed things out, but it punctuated Bobebbie's last event.

Baby didn't care for the day-to-day routine, but became quite excited when the many challenges arose. One such challenge included the greatest deception the hotel ever displayed to both the owner and the president of the franchise. During the slow time, the hotel went against the franchise agreement and would close down its fine dining restaurant to save on expenses. With less than one weeks notice the hotel was forced to host, the owner of the hotel and the president of the franchise for dinner. Baby, staffed the kitchen, planned the meals, and filled the restaurant with shells to look as though they were busy. Waiters, waitresses, maids, houseman, vendors, and friends of the hotel filled the restaurant for a free four-star meal. It cost the hotel thousands of dollars to pull off this charade all so Bootlick and Scam could stay in good graces. Baby would eventually be betrayed by Bootlick and fired for " malfeasance". The liquor cost "appeared out of line" so they assumed she removed wine from the hotel. Never any proof, she sued the nitwits and received a hefty settlement. Now, she is one of the most successful grub and beverage director's in the country.

Jersey, the only true chef the hotel ever hired, also came on board during these glory years. A typical hard-working Ocean City server, he was always doing at least three things at once. Jersey served great food and developed his own young staff with the lowest payroll in the history of the hotel. No one acted surprised knowing that his background of being a Navy Chef, he expected as much from the staff as he did from himself. He put out the best tailgate party ever seen during the professional football seasons. That alone held him in the highest regard for any and all the staff at the hotel. Generously, over the years, he hosted every interested server who enjoyed such an event.

Since Sot's departure there had been a number of short-lived Directors of Sales. Bootlick, once again, asked Japes to help bring stability to this area. Japes recruited, Classee, his old pal from the Harsh' hotels. She brought a much-needed air of class to a somewhat befuddled department. It did not take her long to figure out the players and to use her own magic in accomplishing her goals. Learning from her past and creating a winning culture based on diligent, hard work propelled Classee, her team, and this new wave of second-tier managers to accomplishments not even imagined by the owners. Classee and Japes agreed on how to maximize revenues for the hotel, and the necessity to make any important decisions without Bootlick getting involved. The sales department followed her lead as she brought in servers who she previously worked with to help put heads in beds.

THE BEGINNING OF THE END

The millennium arrived and maybe it involved the alignment of the stars, but one would like to think success reflected the hard work invested by this incredible group of servers. That year the hotel would send the owners over two million dollars above the budgeted profit. There's nothing like a couple of million dollars to bring a big smile to an owners face. This accomplishment, as great as it was, actually paled in comparison to the service recognition the skillful servers would receive. The franchise gave out a handful of awards to hotels that were the best of the best in the world. This "Pinnacle Award" was presented to four hotels that year out of over five thousand worldwide. Typically, the hotels that received such awards maintained high customer satisfaction, high condition of the facility, and incredible physical layouts. Over the years, Japes had formed a good bond with Shuffle-head when he came to inspect the hotel. Japes, not blind to politics, cultivated Shuffle-head's ego by agreeing with and implementing as many of his recommendations as possible. The inspector could make the difference between an average score, a good score, and even an excellent score. The Oasis physical layout, by all standards, stood a notch below the greatest hotels in the system despite the efforts by Chief and his crew. Japes knew the only way to receive this award depended on having the highest customer satisfaction scores in the entire system. The hotel did this, and even to Shuffle-heads surprise they climbed to the top of the mountain. The customer satisfaction scores, which in Japes book and any real hotelier's book, represented the true measure. After all the servers couldn't move the hotel to a new location or build a different type of guest room. They played the cards that were dealt and everything came up aces.

To celebrate with all the servers Japes planned an evening extravaganza highlighting the typical venues this group had frequented. He hired a minibus to transport the managers to the city and forbade anybody to drive a car. On the way Rupee the van driver graciously stopped at the local liquor store. Each server purchased a drink of choice for the half-hour ride into the city. Why not start off with a bang? Japes good friend oversaw the bar at one of the premier restaurants in the city and would host them all. The group enjoyed the best table adjacent to the bar with a perfect view of all the talent the city had to offer. The dinner served on the house and included such meals as tenderloins of beef, veal chops, lobster tails, and even a few burgers for some. The drinks, however, would have to be taken care of by Japes. He knew they were in trouble when Conquer, the visiting builder, ordered a shot of the best tequila for everybody. This round of drinks alone tallied three hundred dollars. After leaving the terrific server, who put up with their shenanigans, with a five hundred dollar gratuity, the gang made way to court-side seats at an NBA game. On the way, the bus took a detour to the infamous Pluto bar for of course a pre-game cocktail. Japes liquor fund had already been depleted, and Bootlick being his typical self asked for a glass of the finest port in the house. The bartender dusted off a dirty old bottle of the worst rotgut anybody had ever seen. The group left him the check. He must have been hammered, as he never spent a nickel on anybody.

They showed up for the game at halftime. In retrospect, it was probably a good thing, as most of the gang, hammered to giggletown, needed time to sober off and gain their bearings. Bootlick never able to do this constantly cheered and clapped for the opposing team. A number of the servers tried to enter the players' locker room, but were abruptly turned away by massive security guards. Smiles used his inebriated charm to heckle the opposing coach from his court side seat throughout the game. To the astonishment of the crowd, he pestered so effectively that even the opposing players started to laugh. The fine honed skills of a hotelier. A few of the servers did not make it inside the stadium spending the second half of the game drinking in local bars. In some instances they were kicked out of the bars and were sitting on the street corner. After gathering everybody together for the trip back Japes encountered a constant chant and a banging on the roof of the van. A vulgar roar of "tit tee bar, tit tee bar, tit tee bar," came to an unstoppable crescendo. Japes, overruled by the gang, were on their way to a strip club. When Smiles asked Japes, "Do you want a piece of me we can go right now?" he knew everyone had had too much to drink. As a few servers trickled from the bus to the doorstep of the strip club, they were of course denied access. In fact, some of the older servers couldn't even get out of their seats to make it to the door. Again, blasted out of his mind, Smiles told Japes while staring at an enormous bouncer "You take him high and I'll take him low". The group schlepped back onto the bus and finally Rupee drove everyone home. Bootlick, upon exiting the vehicle in front of the hotel, dropped his drawers to his knees and peed in the parking lot. There he stood in all his glory the fearless leader who persuaded the gang to drink in such excess that he couldn't even control his own bodily functions. Any respect the servers and especially Japes had for Bootlick was lost that night.

Snub-nose was appointed as the new regional Poobah. She looked and acted just like a bulldog pushing her way into everyone's space. Barely capable of managing a limited service hotel, she, for some unknown reason, had been appointed to do Scam's bidding. The business did not warrant such a position and as a result the beginning of micromanagement and disruption throughout the company began. Snub-nose stuck her nose into everything, even though the hotel far exceeded all goals that were set forth. A formal announcement as to her responsibilities never transpired. Over time all the servers learned that she excelled at being a patented fabricator of the truth just like Scam, and she turned any private communication into her own interpretation for personal gain. This is exactly what this clear thriving world avoided over the past fifteen years. Even Bootlick was rendered useless, as under this new scrutiny he couldn't perform his one task of occupying the executives.

After a number of outings, similar to the basketball trip, Japes and Oh were accused of abusing the hotel trade policy. To start with, there was no trade policy and all the trades or exchanges that Japes and Oh engaged in were approved and endorsed by Bootlick. An unhappy new server lodged the complaint stating that the trades benefited only a few and set a poor example for the rest. Jersey and Oh planned a much smaller outing to go see a comedy show in the city. One of the reasons for the outing intended to console Rupee, the limousine driver, who had lost his son to cancer. Rupee would drive the gang into the city and as a result of an overnight room trade the ten managers would be treated to free drinks and a show in the city. Rupee and his driver were given complimentary tickets to the show purchased by Japes. In exchange, he would make sure all the servers arrived at their homes safely. Upon returning to the hotel a number of the servers were laughing and acting silly, as they had had a great night of fun. The ramifications of this run-of-the-mill outing would forever change the hotel's culture and became known as "The Spanish Inquisition".

Japes, Oh, and Bubblehead were all summoned to the woodshed for a meeting with Bootlick and Snub-nose. A night auditor took it upon himself to write the owners making outrageous accusations in particular stating what Oh, months earlier, had said about screwing a guest's wife and more recently the outing to the comedy show. Bubblehead at the meeting for some reason supported the audit servers' accusations in a hope to get Oh and Japes fired. Bootlick, in his usual fashion, denied any knowledge of the outing and any trades involved. A flat out lie, and although Japes did not plan the outing, he took full responsibility of what transpired emphatically stating that nothing occurred without approval. The hotel periodically would comp guest rooms, and more specifically Japes had full authority to provide free rooms at his own discretion. He reiterated that all the trades the movie theater in particular benefited everyone in the hotel. The particular outing in question, a trip to a comedy show for mature audiences, was totally inappropriate for the ladies. All interested managers, including Bubblehead, were invited and nobody excluded. The situation with Oh and the hotel guest were reviewed at length by Bootlick months' prior to the outing. During this disruption to the hotel, the customer service scores went from an average of ninety to the low fifties. Snub-nose, stuck her nose in where it did not belong, and she did not have the skills to handle the situation. As a result, Japes, Oh, and Bubblehead were summoned to the woodshed two weeks later to face their accuser as to what he wrote in "the letter". The accuser, a part-time night auditor who Japes hired, apparently had aspirations of being the Rooms Executive. He felt that he and Bubblehead could run the room operation in a better more professional manner. This little political coup became quite transparent for what it claimed. The accuser never showed up for the meeting as there was no substance to the accusations and he had simply lied. Bubblehead would never recover from his betrayal of all the managers and eventually would leave with his tail tucked between his legs. Snub-nose, unable to apologize, stated that even though they did nothing wrong the fact that it appeared as though they did something wrong was the issue. It became all about appearances not reality. This event symbolized exactly what Japes father always warned him about. It is not what people say it's what they do that matters. In this case, it's not what they did it's what other people say.

As the years went by, the woodshed meetings in general had taken on an entirely different agenda. It, to a certain extent, related to 911 as this tragic day forever changed the landscape for Hotels worldwide. Bootlick would often refer to the hotel servers as lemmings who would

207

follow him around as if he were the Pied Piper. This total lack of respect for his coworkers would normally come to the forefront during an outside event such as a social gathering with the Chamber of Commerce. Scam also became quite disrespectful when referring to servers who worked at the hotel. At one meeting he wanted to know what was wrong with Mildred, an elderly housekeeper, because he noticed that she shook all the time. Japes informed him that she had a mild case of diabetes and sometimes she would shake. She was, however, one of the best workers and most loyal servers the hotel ever employed. Scam didn't care for some odd reason he wanted to push her out of the hotel. Japes ignored this ridiculous request and thought these two don't even act like hoteliers. Something from the outside world must have influenced them, as their leadership looked more like a cancer than guidance. Bewildered by this behavior and hoping it represented just a phase with no real substance behind it, he remained positive. By this time, his dystrophy progressed to the point whereby basic routines challenged him, and the brass was fully aware.

It started many years earlier, but Japes being a third generation server and liking the situation he thrived in, chose to ignore the truth. The truth being Scam embodied a taker and over the years would continuously reinforce his lack of respect for him. The first hint of his taking occurred at a year-end review when Bootlick and Japes were detailing capital expenses. Japes noticed two ten thousand dollar expenditures for new furniture in the lobby bar. The hotel had not purchased any new furniture for the lobby bar that year, but the invoices had been approved by Scam. When informing the corporate controller of the situation he was told not to be concerned, as Scam would have the final word with any capital improvements. Apparently, there were no checks and balances, and the invoice "Barber Associates" received constant approval. Also, during the first year he achieved a small bonus by reaching certain goals. At the year-end review Scam informed him that he did not qualify for this and hung up the telephone. Japes, pissed off, dealt directly with the controller and finally, after realizing that the goals were clearly met, it was decided he would get paid. Bullying a subordinate had become second nature to Scam.

Scam often called requesting Japes to hire new associates. Early on, forced to hire Scams niece and to keep an eye on her, he became leery. Placing her in the maintenance department, as her appearance and attitude would have destroyed the professional and highly skilled front office, he sort of complied. It did not take long, however, for her true colors to shine through as the line servers realized she was a thief. One-day the local police department reported that a guest had his wallet stolen, which included tickets to a basketball game, a credit card, and three hundred dollars in cash. Scams niece, the last employee in the room bragged about attending the game. Managing to keep her out of the authorities' hands and miraculously finding the wallet and credit card outside the hotel proved just enough to send her on her way, unfortunately, she would regularly be seen over the years as her family's company continued to complete capital improvements to the building. Hiring the town assessor's daughter because she was a "friend of the hotel" proved too much, so he refused. The daughter eventually ended up working for Ho-hum as a server, and the town assessor enjoyed a free membership to the pool.

When Capes suggested and eventually accomplished turning the pool into a new ballroom Scam took full recognition not only for the implementation of the structure and its design, but also for the idea itself. During a review, when Capes brought up his accomplishments, Scam and Snub-nose just looked at him and shook their heads saying how disappointed they were with him taking the credit. This clear act of idea piracy compounded, when Scam in all his glory took full credit for the standard-bearer award in Sin City. Standing up in front of his peers and hundreds of hotel owners from around the world, Little Cesar convinced the owner that this success reflected his efforts.

As time went on Scam became bolder and bolder in his desire to take from the hands that fed him. Japes worked hard for a number of months to get the right vendor that would put a beautiful kiosk in the lobby. After negotiations, and the agreement to build a custom mahogany cabinet, the deal was done. The only thing left called for the vendor to take the contract over to Scam for his signature. Receiving a call from the vendor telling him that Scam needed five thousand dollars in cash or he would not sign the contract demoralized Japes. The vendor, rightfully irate, clearly knowing this represented a bribe wanted to know to whom could he speak. Japes sat at his desk shaking his head and told the gentleman that he would have to talk to the owners. He apologized profusely for Scams behavior, but knew that nothing would happen even after the vendor made the call. Scam, talked his way out of it and went about his business as if nothing ever happened.

All of this would pale in comparison as to how he and his associate would take the owners on the development of a sister property. Scam used his old practices, sharing the bids with his friend and this time he undercut a one million dollar quote for nine hundred and ninety nine thousand dollars and throughout the process of renovating the new property he changed the scope of work. Scam would oftentimes be seen walking with the owner stating that this had been done and that had been rebuilt when in fact nothing was done at all.

He cried like a baby when, Barber Associates, was shut down by the state inspectors. They had not cleared working areas of a hazardous substance and as a result exposed hundreds of both servers and guests at risk. The worst thing that can happen to a hotel is to have it close. They were forced to close this hotel, and the owners would spend over a half million dollars in fines and legal fees before all was said and done. It makes a server scratch their head as to how Scam could convince the owners that he held no blame. He personified one of the most gifted fabricators of the truth that Japes would ever deal with and the owners possessing so much wealth let it all slide.

The end of the Oasis came in a way that Japes never dreamed of. He sat in the cafeteria one day and noticed dozens of flyers scattered throughout. Curious as to what that entailed, he began to read an excerpt from a neighboring state's newspaper. The writing involved the building of a new hotel and the article included the name of Scam as one of the new owners. The rumor mill ran wild with accusations of Scam using company assets, in this case corporate sales and marketing, to drum up business for a new venture. Was he leaving the company? Did the owners for whom they all had worked for so many years have any idea what was going on? On the outside it seemed to be quite a conflict, and surely the owners would have given him their blessing after all they had been through together. Bootlick and Ho-hum were the ones that sent out copies of the article to all. These two hated Scam and his myriad of hypocritical behavior as much as anyone. Casanova, who left the company months earlier, got wind of the changes, and telephoned Japes to see if it was true. Japes forwarded a copy of the article from the website provided to him by Ho-hum with a note that he couldn't believe Scam would be leaving the company after so many years. Well, Casanova, unbeknownst to Japes, had an axe to grind with Scam for what was probably a legitimate reason so he forwarded the e-mail to the owner of the company. The owners had no clue what Scam had been up to, and in fact the article placed him on the proverbial hot seat thus jeopardizing his coveted, little chair. Years later Casanova, now a college professor, said, "If I caused him even a little discomfort it was worth it".

It took Scam over a year with some incredibly vicious tactics, including cutting Japes incentive plan, and not accommodating his ambulatory needs, but he finally got him to move on. He blamed Japes directly for putting him in an awkward position with the owners when in fact he had merely relayed an article. If Japes ever intended on dropping a dime on the little homuncule he held a lot more ammunition than a copy of an obscure newspaper article. He never would have exposed Scam, as this act flew in the face of what Japes believed in, and belied his own personal philosophy. Bootlick would not survive even a year without Japes to manage the hotel for him. He would be relegated to a figurehead position in sales and in short order forced out of the company altogether. A decade has gone by and the hotel has never recognized success even close to what the gang delivered.

The Crossroads

Japes had a decision to make, should he pursue another position similar to what he had done his entire career or should he try something new. As fate would have it, the relationships that he built with his subordinates, owners, and bosses over the years would pay dividends. His old pal All-in, from the Harsh days, a successful executive and in charge of four hotels around the city, knew Japes struggled in a tough situation and suggested a change of career. It would be drastically different from what he had done his entire life, but he could remain working in a hotel and more importantly, he would have the security of collaborating with an honest server. He decided to take the position as a controller even though he would spend his time working with the dreaded Flatheads. All-in provided Japes and his family a corporate long-term policy, which upon retirement, would take care of their needs. A good transition for him as his health continued to decline to the point of using a walker, and his new position did not require him to move about. Blessed to have parents who taught him to be a lifelong learner, in only a few months he performed all the functions necessary to do the job.

The hotel, situated in a tertiary market and not achieving the same level of service or maintaining the same standards he once enjoyed, worried him. The socioeconomic climate at the Oasis Hotel proved as good as it gets, the socioeconomic climate at the new property proved as tough as it gets. For the operational managers, supervision appeared difficult, as the line staff came from challenging backgrounds and lived in tough neighborhoods. The hotel did not have the same feeling or open communication channels that Japes had been accustomed to when developing and nourishing his staff. His new role, purely financial, entailed spending literally eight hours a day looking at numbers and interpreting various spreadsheets. For the rest of his hotel career, he looked at spreadsheets, financial statements, and tried to limit any liability exposure for the owners. A new world for Japes, and all the mysterious terminology used by the bean counters over the years became as clear as day. Working on pro formas and assisting All-in evaluate numerous hotels for acquisition, consumed a fair amount of his time. The joke around the office with his fellow Flatheads, whenever a question surfaced, the answer always involved creating a new spreadsheet. They would refer to this unrelenting task as mental masturbation. Japes mentor, Gladstone, a lifelong Flathead, a bit eccentric, but knowledgeable and well respected within the hotel accounting community was charming.

This new existence, a far cry from what Japes pursued his entire life, challenged his abilities. A doer and a motivator throughout his career, the Flatheads viewed everything in the rearview mirror and in many cases looked at situations that occurred months and even years in the past. It seemed easy to be right when you didn't have to be proactive. The bean counters simply accounted for what other servers had done. The new company, laden with CPAs, accountants, and of course the lawyers, unveiled the ugly world of business dealing not only with making money and protecting one's assets, but most importantly treating people simply as numbers. If the company could save money in any way by eliminating costs than they would do so. It did not matter if these costs affected one or every server who worked for them. For example, the hotel for years had eliminated the cafeteria and made the employees pay for the lunch. For most of these servers it represented the only good meal that they would get and the cost was minimal to maintain a strong and healthy workforce. They did not care, as the bottom line would improve incrementally and they in turn would be compensated.

Perhaps the greatest disregard for fellow servers involved determining the cost of their health care. By and large, the servers who worked in the hotel were on the low end of the pay scale, but they were required to pay the same amount for health insurance as the executives. In many cases the health insurance cost them between fifteen and twenty percent of their annual pay. For All-in, this became a relentless battle convincing the company to pay any portion of the premium. If the owners had their way they would have charged the entire premium to the employee and for most this represented forty percent of their entire pay. Japes believed this showed greed at its worst. Ironically, the executives who worked directly with the owner at the corporate office did not have to pay anything for their health insurance. The parent corporation thought it fit to take care of this benefit, but they in turn would not be so moral. Not a good model for a long-lived successful organization.

The President of the new company was quite a character, a pure Flathead with limited education but great success. Shekelhound, a Northlander, started out as a bank teller, a natural with numbers, and for most of his career acted as a regional controller for the largest hotel chain in the world. He in essence founded this small company while speaking with the owner many years ago during a vacation in the tropics. Shekelhound persuaded the owner to let him take over the management of his hotel and over the years acquired and built a half-dozen more. Although, not well educated, he artfully held his own in the boardroom and delivered millions of dollars in profit to the ownership. Early on, Japes learned that Shekelhound carved himself a great golden parachute and if he wanted could retire at any time. Perhaps this influenced his behavior, but Japes could not help but laugh as Shekelhound likened himself to a duck. He stated, "I fly in every month for this regional meeting and crap on everybody then leave." Japes liked Shekelhound very much as he was "a natural" at what he did and a born leader. The only man Japes worked with who became so successful, earning nothing more than a 10th grade education impressed him. Despite his position in the company he insisted on having two bottles of vodka placed in his room. He consumed one of them at the hotel, and he took the other home. Wow!

Unlike the other hotels, this one came filled with professionals who dealt directly with ownership. Japes introduction to the crowd revolved around a monthly poker game which All-in organized for Shekelhound. Shekelhound, a great poker player, who not only loved to win, he, also consumed an entire bottle of vodka during the game. If he felt like it, after the game, he persuaded the boys to crawl down to the bar and have a nightcap. The game, attended by a few friends of the hotel, included Tar, a private architect who worked with Shekelhound for many years, Bowser, a local barrister, Gladstone the regional controller, Bailey a sales director, and various other managers from sister properties. There were a large number of games played and one could even win a few hundred dollars if he possessed some skills. The challenge for Japes came not so much from the games as keeping pace with the drinking. All the players except for a few would consume an entire bottle of liquor each. The traditional food served with the game appeared as eclectic as the group that gathered, including enormous shrimp cocktail, hot dogs, pizza, and assorted mixed nuts. One found it necessary to consume some food or else the chances of passing out were greatly enhanced. Over the years, Japes had done his best work in the cafeterias, he felt certain that Shekelhound used the poker game to do his management. You find out a lot about a server while playing a game of chance and when you are drinking. To say the least everybody loosened up and one's character would always show through when playing for real money. Bailey and Japes were the rookies to this game, and although they kept from passing out they had no clue how to play the exotic poker games continuously introduced. Shekelhound, like a hawk with his eye on all participants, made certain the pot remained properly anted and that everyone received the correct payout. He hated a cheater and he usually won the most money.

The perspective of these professionals, both fascinating and refreshing to Japes, opened his eyes. Highly respected and working with many different people on a regular basis paled to the exposure Japes enjoyed with literally hundreds of thousands of patrons during his hoteliers life giving him a distinctive background. A relatively mundane story to Japes concerning hotel behavior triggered belly gurgling laughter and total enthusiasm by the group. On the other hand, Japes, fascinated with legal proceedings as well as various designs associated with the industry learned much. The true hotelier stays in the business because he loves it regardless of the income. Like anything there is a trade-off and from where Japes sat, wanting many experience in life, it proved the only field to be in. In his mind the professionals, although they made significant incomes, had not enjoyed the multitude of life experiences that only a hotelier can have when dealing with the public day in and day out. There was no basic routine for the hotel servers' as each and every guest had their own specific needs and required differing attention. Japes enjoyed the poker games, confirming to himself that working in such a server filled environment rewarded him with a culture not enjoyed by the others. Life involves many choices, but the real key is how one feels. The endless nuance of active listening and appropriate action brings gratification far beyond that of personal gain.

The world from the accountant's perspective proved to be rather boring. The wonderful operational stories that excited Japes every day would become few and far between. The mental masturbation involved while looking at the same thing in a multitude of different formulas and utilizing algorithms proved educational but not fulfilling. Japes could not resist so he became more involved with the operation of the hotel. He found he could perform all the accounting duties necessary during the first two hours of his workday, leaving him the remaining hours to do whatever he wanted. Spending a lot of his time meandering around the property and observing the behavior of the staff, made him feel good. A difficult property to manage at the level of customer service, which Japes had grown accustomed to, confirmed his transition. Although the hotel employed many fine workers and a number of dedicated managers, the culture appeared different. The hotel accepted service and standards, reminding him of driving a Chevy rather than a Mercedes. The old saying "How can I fly with the eagles when I am surrounded by crows" certainly felt true at this unique location. The hotel stood unique in that it encompassed two complete buildings connected by an enclosed walkway lovingly referred to as the tube. It took a server at least ten minutes to go from one end of the building adjacent to the pool to the other end of the building past the restaurant. Upon arrival, guests were often times instructed by the guest service agent to get back in their car and drive to the other building, as it would be easier for them to drive to the guest room instead of walking the entire length of the building. The hotel, a maintenance nightmare, operated two of everything, including electricity supply, heating furnaces, water supply, and air-conditioning.

One-day in the fall, a terrible rainstorm besieged the area, and the wind blew at fifty mph. The fire alarms went off throughout the property and the staff discovered an enormous water leak in the middle of the building. Apparently, a portion of a roof vent broke away and the rain poured directly into the electrical room, which provided power to the hotel. Japes had never seen anything like this, as there were three inches of water on the floor of the room, which housed thousands of watts of electricity. Upon arrival, he informed the fire chief of the situation and recommended that they not walk into that room. The chief told him to get out of the way he wore rubber boots and appeared unphased. There must be something in the drinking water, thought Japes, as this clown walked into an electrical room that could kill him in an instant without shutting off the power. Eventually, this is what they did and it was pure luck that the fireman did not get lit up like a Christmas tree.

A FEW PLAYERS

There were a few true hoteliers at the hotel that enjoyed a career in the industry and for varying circumstances also ended up at this Crossroads Hotel. The front office, Japes forte and where he got his start in the business, was managed by a bunch of kids. Although All-in did the best he could to oversee this group it became painfully obvious to Japes that they left a lot of money on the table. The youngest of the bunch, Cleopatra, an attractive server who over the next ten years would run the front office, had a lot going for her and worked her way up from a vocational school with high recommendations from her professors. Her story would be typical of every potentially talented young manager that Japes encountered during his tenure at the Crossroads. Like most good-looking twenty-year-olds Cleopatra courted a boyfriend who pursued her wherever she went. Unfortunately, due to the circumstances surrounding many of the servers in that community, even at her humble earnings she became the breadwinner. Inevitably, she got pregnant and gave birth to a beautiful baby out of wedlock. A well-known story rumored that her boyfriend, a drug dealer, placed her into compromising situations. She eventually would leave the partner, but engaged hotel resources in her subculture for many shakey transactions. The biggest pimp in the area constantly tried to get Cleopatra to join his stable. She never succumbed to his pursuit, but arrangements were made so that his existing stable could walk the halls and use the guest rooms for free. Never a pimp, she did, however, enable him to push twenty-dollar hookers throughout the hotel. A far cry from what Japes experienced thirty years ago when he started out.

The Chef, Bloodshot, an accomplished cook, had no formal training, but unlike many of the chefs Japes worked with he could not handle his drinking. Bloodshot, a true Red-eye server, produced enormous holiday brunches that fed close to two thousand happy patrons. He cooked during brunch to keep up with the demand; whereby common practice would be to have everything prepared ahead of time. He drank so much during the day management eventually received complaints that he smelled of booze. He shook so bad he could not hold a glass of water without spilling it. Bloodshot despite this terrible disease remained well liked by most of the staff and only after an investigation did the depth of his problem come to light.

Nobody would drop a dime on Bloodshot unless something drastic occurred. Of course, like most things when a group waits until something drastic happens it's just too late. The end came for Bloodshot in Japes mind when he heard that Bloodshot left his beautiful four-year old son alone as he slept passed out on the couch. It had nothing to do with the workplace, but it spotlighted the sign that any healthy person would take to make a change. Bloodshot soon thereafter began to miss shifts and not function under even the easiest of circumstances. He was helped out the door, but in reality he drank everything away, including his marriage, and his career.

The Director of Sales, Jupiter, a true mentsch from Empire City, epitomized a seasoned veteran with years of experience in hotel sales. She ended up at the Crossroads Hotel in large part as a result of circumstances outside of work and made the best out of this dysfunctional organization. To her benefit, the company, laden with accountants, employed not one executive or owner that had a clue about sales and marketing. All-in paved his way as a front office server and even he had limited experience with sales and marketing. Jupiter survived despite her endless battles with Mara on how to best sell the hotel. When you do not know what it takes to sell a hotel and the operational servers do not give a damn, inevitably you will be fighting an uphill battle. This environment would turn even the most optimistic server into a realist and eventually into a skeptic. The hotel would not thrive financially, but it performed well enough for the owners to make a little cash. Jupiter acted like a little pit bull when it came to defending her positions, and she worked harder than most sales servers to smooth out the relentless operational issues.

Survivor, the Food and Beverage Manager, mainly ran the banquets department, but would eventually also run the restaurant and the kitchen. She toiled in the industry for many years and worked in other hotels as a banquet manager. Survivor created a loyal following and she knew how to keep her peeps happy. Always defending their behavior whenever questioned, even in an upscale hotel this was a challenging position, and at the Crossroads it proved even more so. She kept her core group of housemen and servers at the hotel for decades while maintaining a steady level of service. In its heyday the Crossroads hosted in excess of one hundred weddings per year with two extravagant spiral staircases as the centerpiece to the ballroom foyer. This one niche market within the hotel and within the surrounding communities provided a much-needed jolt of publicity. Survivor dealt with a lot of rough characters, and if not for the many new competitors in the market the Crossroads would still be doing hundreds of weddings every year.

Bluree, the engineer, worked in many hotels throughout the city and had exceptional knowledge of all the trades and safety codes. Focusing in on one thing at a time proved to be impossible for Bluree. If he said it once he said it a million times "I just want to do the right thing," pertaining to any project the hotel undertook. For example, the building sprung a leak on an exterior wall in the back section of one of the wings. The outside displayed a brick façade and a standard roof. The owners received a bid to patch the roof and the adjacent flashing along with repointing all of the bricks in that area. Bluree emphatically informed Japes and All-in that the entire roof needed to be replaced, that the windows in that section of the wing needed to be replaced, and that one quarter of the entire exterior bricks should be replaced. The contractor submitted a price of fourteen thousand dollars for the first scenario and one hundred and sixty five thousand dollars for the second scenario. Bluree relentless called for management to do the right thing, but frankly, he acted out of his mind. No guarantee that either scenario would solve the problem, the owners certainly were not going to rebuild half the hotel over a water leak. When, after years of service, Bluree gained other employment this incessant pursuit of rebuilding everything cost him his job. A smart server who meant well, but talked so fast about so many different topics in such a short period of time that it proved impossible to keep up.

When first purchased the Crossroads Hotel enjoyed significant profits. Taken out of foreclosure for a price half what it cost to build, Japes learned from this new group what people of means could do that the average man could not. Although it was not an upscale facility, it certainly attracted the middle-of-the-road characters that one would expect to see at these income levels. Perhaps one of the most unique pieces of business that Japes became involved with occurred not only at the crossroads hotel, but also at its sister property in the city. The company contracted with the state for the housing of many that had no homes and were considered section eight. As a hotelier, he was shocked, that even this midscale hotel would allow such business in the doors. He told Shekelhound that the position of the hotel within the market would suffer greatly as these customers would cause security problems galore. They would be seen with small hibachi grills cooking outside the rooms along with drug dealers, estranged fathers', and social workers constantly trafficking the hotel. The corporate travelers, which brought in the bulk of the revenues to the hotel, would be offended by such a boondoggle, and eventually would find accommodations elsewhere. Shekelhound affectionately referred to these rooms as the "Klinger rooms" from the TV series "Mash". Over a two-year period the two hotels would receive over two million dollars in revenue from the state, which paid one hundred dollars per night per room. Japes thought that this business was wrong on so many levels he did not know where to begin. How could the state, possibly spend that much every month for a mother and child who were homeless to live in a hotel? Surely, there must be a more economical means by which these displaced families could be taken care of. Managers in the hotel did the best they could to handle this daycare center and home for the weary. Bluree, constantly attended to floods from overflowing bathtubs in their rooms, and Jupiter acted as a surrogate mother giving them food and aiding them with basic day-to-day survival. As predicted, many of the regular customers left the hotel never to return. This highlighted the difference between a true hotel company and a company run by accountants and number crunchers. For the short term, it looked like the hotel performed incredibly well, and the executives were making fistfuls of dollars in bonus money. But, if one were to take a longer view of the profitability, it would be obvious that the loss in the positioning of the hotel would end up costing the company in lost revenue. Already a tough hotel to manage, with these short-sited decisions it appeared nearly impossible.

Another group, filling the bill of shortsighted incremental revenue, included the infamous Magazine group. These clients contracted a large number of rooms at twenty-nine dollars per night with as many as six sleeping in the doubles. Every misfit from all parts of the country would descend upon the hotel. These knuckleheads would be dropped off in various communities within a ten-mile radius of the hotel. They would then go door to door trying to sell magazines and various periodicals to local residents. Most of the guests, from low-income families, were sold a bill of goods with the promise of traveling the country and finding fortune. In essence, they were poorly trained door-to-door salesmen who could barely squeak out a living and lived day-to-day. With such a large number of frustrated people it inevitably escalated into a problem. One Sunday the group created so much noise that Throwback, the manager on duty, became alarmed forcing him to call the local police department to stop the disturbance. Throwback, Japes old housekeeper from the Oasis Hotel, had decided to jump ship and work for All-in. Well, this incident presented a first for Throwback, so he called All-in on that Sunday as the hotel looked more like a boxing ring than it did a place of business. Arriving ahead of the police, All-in and Throwback were confronted with four large men yelling and screaming causing an uproar. All-in looked at the largest of the group and stated "Let's go right now and settle this once and for all!" The others backed down and within the hour the entire group vacated the premises. Throwback, the next day, told Japes, that if they had gone at it, he and All-in would have gotten pummeled. Constituting a far cry from what the Oasis Hotel cultivated for so many years, he hoped to introduce his own magic.

To bring the team closer together Japes planned an outing that afternoon to a baseball game. Japes, All-in, Throwback, Bloodshot, Bowser, Gladstone, and Stumblebum were all picked up in a limousine and taken to Fenway Park for the night. Staying true to their colors, they all bellied up to a bar and pounded beers for a couple of hours before hopping over to the park. A former employee managed the club level and provided everybody an inside look at the park, inviting the gang to see how a national treasure operated behind the scenes. All-in being the great giver, provided Japes, Gladstone, and Throwback quadruple shots of gin all night long. The three became so rowdy that All-in and the others sat in a different section of the club. Upon returning to the hotel, it had been predetermined that everybody would stay and not drive home. Throwback, completely legless at the time, decided to drive his truck home despite everybody yelling at him. Fortunately, he did not kill anyone on his ride home, although he was stopped for driving in the wrong lane. Fate kept him safe that night. Times have changed greatly over the years and the penalties for drinking and driving are rightfully extremely severe. Japes would never be involved in another drinking and driving boondoggle.

As crazy as this escapade transpired, it paled in comparison to All-in's annual casino trip. He would hire a bus every fall and load the bus up with enough beer and sandwiches so that every server could eat and drink their way into a complete stupor. The bus ride took about an hour and a half and the thirty or so servers would easily consume ten cases of beer. All-in, not wanting to appear cheap, gave everybody a one-dollar scratch ticket as a giveaway. Upon arrival, each server would visit the administrative office and receive a free chance at the casinos keno drawing. Of course, this highlighted All-in's favorite vice as he and a bunch of managers would go to the horse racing parlor and bet on as many races as they possibly could. The remaining servers scattered throughout the casino playing their favorite games of chance. Although this did not represent a traditional form of team building, it certainly separated the professional drinkers from the amateurs. In all the years the hotel made this trip no server won more than a couple of hundred dollars and of course most lost money. The entire group stayed at the Crossroads upon returning in the wee hours of the night. It evolved into a point of interest, for those who could still move about, as to which server would not quite make it into a guest room and required assistance getting to bed.

To keep morale high, All-in also planned summer outings to baseball games for the entire gang. He took everybody to the AA ballpark located just minutes from the hotel. A great venue to watch the future stars of major league baseball and no beer line. These small ballparks created a fun atmosphere for managers to bond, acting as a platform for everyone to talk. The baseball was not the primary reason for going. Of course, after the game, many of the managers would hop around the corner to a local pub and continue drinking until they had their fill. As this planned event cost only a fraction what it cost to go to a major-league park, the group made many trips.

THE APPOINTMENT

Shekelhound ruled over the hotel division and all of its development for nearly two decades. He intimated, during the infamous poker games, that he planned to retire and this would probably be his last year of running the division. He was sixty-five years old with a number of health issues and he had a golden parachute worth one and a half million dollars. During one of his less sober moments, he divulged how much he liked traveling and managing the hotels so he thought maybe he would not retire. Flintstone, who reported directly to the VP of Finance, decided to mention this comment to his boss during Shekelhound's visit. The next day Shekelhound, summoned by the Real Estate President, Scrooge, to immediately return to the corporate office in the Badlands, faced the music. Scrooge, a callus Bull, had already made plans to get Shekelhound out of the company and he would be damned if he was to stay another day. Shekelhound always believed that All-in instigated this quick dismissal, as he stood next in line to take over the hotel operations. In fact, Shekelhound became indignant when he found out all of his signing privileges at the hotel the company owned in the Badland Region were taken away. Shekelhound, although he had retired, thought he would be able to eat and drink at the hotel at no charge for the rest of his life. He would never speak to anybody associated with the hotels ever again. Some of these servers he had worked with for thirty years.

Within a week, Scrooge, promoted All-in to President of the Hotel Division and later, since he liked playing games with the organizational chart, he changed the title to Executive Vice President of Hotel operations. Whatever the title, All-in now in charge of four hotels assumed the responsibility of adding to the portfolio. In the past, Shekelhound received compensation when the company sold any of the hotels. They sold the property in the Islands for thirty five million dollars and Shekelhound received a cash payment equal to one percent of the sale. He also received compensation for the sale of the property they owned in Graniteville. It proved great for Shekelhound, but foolish on the part of Scrooge, as the Graniteville property would have continued to make millions for the company if not sold. This exposed a new, unfamiliar greed of how to line one's pockets never considering the best outcome for the company. All-in would not partake in any such windfalls, as Scrooge hated to pay bonuses or even operational incentives that were common practice throughout the industry. Scrooge did not have an ounce of respect for the hotel servers', acted extremely condescending and single-minded with his financial hyperbole, and nestled himself so far up the owner's butt that he could do no wrong. He would be sure to line his own pockets at the expense of any and all of the hotel servers. This created the antithesis of a culture necessary to build participation.

After his promotion, All-in went right to work and found a great hotel at a price well below market. All-in had done his homework, had a manager lined up to run the hotel, had a lawyer ready to do the closing, had an engineer review the physical structure, and knew the market was growing with little room for added competition. It seemed like the perfect deal, but Scrooge informed the group that they would not be purchasing the hotel not because it wouldn't make money, but because it wouldn't make enough money. It took years to find an acceptable hotel and although this one met the criteria set forth by Scrooge he arbitrarily decided it was not good enough. The problem with having an accountant run a business is that they look at everything in the rearview mirror. Displaying no imagination or tolerance for risk of any type represented boredom. Jumping at the chance to purchase the hotel, another group, ten years later thrives under its new flag making the owners rich. To Japes and All-in it did not seem like a difficult decision, but after listening to Scrooge talking in circles about market penetration and return on investment one would think they were doing something that had never been done before. In the end, it emphasized Scrooge's display of power and control.

Gladstone, the server who dropped the dime on Shekelhound, who everyone thought enjoyed a good reputation with the corporate offices, appeared to be in line for a promotion. Gladstone assumed that he and All-in would be in charge of the Hotel Division including operations and development. An interesting man, born a Downeaster, he represented a pure flathead in a large body with a quirky clown-like demeanor. His reputation, as a mad professor was misplaced for his actual intellect proved to be much higher than his responsibilities as a regional executive. Scrooge, however, did not treat Gladstone with any respect and in fact made fun of him as a result of his slow responses during meetings. He made Gladstone look incompetent like a high school bully picking on someone who they couldn't quite understand. Despite this, Gladstone based on his contributions to the organization and substantial background felt optimistic about being promoted along with his friend All-in. This did not happen as Scrooge, although stating he wanted to grow the company, in essence cut back on the executive positions. He wanted the money for himself plain and simple. Gladstone, devastated by this maneuver, within the year would leave the company for a wonderful position in a much larger hotel organization. He's one of the few normal servers despite his demeanor that Japes worked with in his career.

All-in would not let this stop him from growing the company and achieving success for himself and his family. Visiting and compiling financial evaluations of dozens of different hotels throughout the region and the country became routine. The process grew more involved and more cumbersome than All-in had anticipated, as he regularly found promising projects, but the financing wouldn't work or the return looked too low. Oftentimes, he found a good project only to be outbid by larger corporations looking for much lower returns on their investments. Searching for the home run, with a high rate of return on the investment, created a high hurdle. Throughout this process, Japes informed All-in that the best returns on investment are limited service hotels which have less risk, less overhead, less operational expense, and have easier exit strategies. The marching orders, however, were to find a full-service hotel in a great location, which returned greater monies. These situations were few and far between as the industry evolved and investors realized that this scenario constituted a hard way to make a buck. All-in would do as directed and continued to look for this needle in a haystack. At one point, All-in gave Japes a lead on a hotel for sale in the heart of the city. An old hotel with no franchise affiliation and only one hundred rooms with an asking price of $6 million for an all-cash deal presented a windfall. To Japes, this looked like a no-brainer as the land alone valued at least six million dollars without any building on it. Furthermore, the location, surrounded by government offices and sporting venues appeared ideal. Scrooge would not even entertain the idea of doing a financial analysis. The hotel sold for the asking price and is today an extremely successful boutique hotel returning millions of dollars annually to the owners. Japes suggested All-in look at "Rearview Hotels", then maybe the owners would bite. If there was no history for the bean counters to look at then projecting out into the future became impossible. How the hell did these so called developers get to where they are?

Much to everyones' surprise, All-in discovered the perfect property a Marion Hotel, considered to be the best franchise in the country. Japes toured the area, and All-in with the help of Bailey conducted all the due diligence for the revenue side of the business. The facility reminded Japes of the Mountain High Hotel that he worked in many years ago. Situated in a great location surrounded by corporate offices with limited competition the hotel had been updated, and although the kitchen looked warn the remaining structure appeared in excellent shape. Inevitably there would be competition, and Japes only hesitation should be remedied when considering the asking price. If no new competition entered the market area than the twenty five million dollar price seemed fair. Again, the bean counters focused in on the past and the history as opposed to the future. Japes, All-in, and Low spent a few days at the hotel to get the lay of the land. Low assumed Gladstone's position, although he did not have quite the same responsibilities. The three were sitting at the lobby bar one evening quietly discussing the purchase of the hotel and came to the conclusion that the sale was actually going to happen. It had been years of work by many servers, but most of the responsibility lay squarely on the shoulders of All-in and Low. Low so excited about the purchase that on a dare, he performed a perfect headstand in the middle of the bar. All-in and Japes promised that everything that happened at the hotel would stay at the hotel, but upon returning to the Crossroads they couldn't help but share this hilarious event. Low, a conservative server who played everything close to the vest, standing on his head in public appeared more than just a little out of character. This act symbolized the great fun in reaching their goal.

The actual closing characterized one of the most memorable events Japes participated in while working for the group at the Crossroads Hotel. The group of executives, including fifteen professionals, half of whom were from the selling company and half of whom were from the Crossroads, all gathered in the "War Room" at the Marion Hotel. Scrooge contributed to the purchase of the hotel via a conference call and would not physically see the property for over a year. The groups progressed through the various steps necessary to purchase such a facility with the lawyers and accountants checking off each item along the way. Details such as liquor licenses, inventories, cash banks, and various vendor contracts were all handled one after another. All-in created a good working relationship with the president of the selling company and agreed on a few small points to expedite the process. During one of these minor steps, Scrooge brought the entire room to a complete silence as he went on a tirade over the speakerphone. He told the president of the selling company that he already screwed him on the depreciation and that they would not assume any of the receivables. By pure luck, the president of the selling company did not pull the plug on the entire deal after such a display. The receivables, insignificant, represented an item that All-in and he agreed upon earlier. He proved to be a big server and let little Scrooge have his way. Obvious to all in the room that Scrooge found it necessary to flex his muscle, he instead exposed his severe difficulty in making a decision. The deal, finally consummated, the entire staff rejoiced by drinking themselves into drunken stupors at one of the local pubs. The event had been a complete fiasco. All-in lead the horse to water, but he almost would not drink. Despite Scrooge everyone felt that the transaction constituted a good deal for both the seller and the buyer. The hotel proved to be a good investment with returns close to what All-in and Low forecasted. Years later, however, the hotel showed declining profits as new competition entered the market and management was not prepared. This of course happened after the team had been dismantled.

The group made a substantial contribution to the growth of the company and continued to work on other projects. Low, despite all of his hard work decided to leave the organization and returned to his prior employer with an equity position. Capitalizing on this, the corporate office decided that his position would be filled with a Flathead halfway across the country. All-in would have to make do, as the replacement in no way held the qualifications to help the group. Japes and the other controllers who worked in the regional office were paid a visit by the corporate controller and vice president of finance. They were informed that the entire organization was evolving and they would report directly to the home office. Japes and his peers were treated so poorly and with such little respect that he did the only thing he could and laughed at them. Apparently, they had just gotten a little taste of what All-in behind-the-scenes dealt with for the past year. Scrooge proved relentless in berating of others, including the VP of Finance whom he brought to tears. Not long after this organizational change, All-in slipped into Japes office, closed the door, and informed him he was leaving the company. He could not listen to Scrooge any longer as he incessantly berated him, speaking to him as if he was a third class citizen. It became so bad that All-in stood ready to resign even without a whisper of a new job. Fortunately, All-in developed relationships the same as Japes had done throughout his career. A previous owner recruited him for the job of his life at a fabulous hotel in the heart of Sin City. All-in felt bad that he brought Japes aboard and abandoned him, but Japes felt All-in had rescued him from a terrible situation. Japes had been around the block and knew there were many Scrooges in the world, and he would deal with this one in his own way. Besides, Japes felt extremely gratified, that All-in learned the biggest lesson of all and that his relationships had in turn rescued him from a terrible situation.

THAT DOG DON'T HUNT

Shekelhound said that nobody could survive Scrooge as he relentlessly bellowed in the boardroom and ultimately wanted to be President of the entire company. Shekelhound proved correct as Scrooge maneuvered his way to the top of the heap laying waste to the corporate lawyer and many who had been with the company for decades. The appointment of Pan-face to be President of the Hotel Division came as no surprise to Japes. Pan-face, the living definition of "a suit" from a long line of pure bread Kiva's, slid in through the back door. A suit represented one, who dresses the part, was well enough educated to converse on many different topics, politically motivated, and never took a stand for or supported any subordinate. The truly good suits took crap from everyone and kept on smiling. Keeping employed and making as much money as possible for as long as they could, defined their existence.

Left with a pure bureaucracy, the team moved forward with literally no leadership. The manager of the crossroads, Bombay, who All-in recruited a few years back, left to his own devises, like Japes fended for himself. The two got along well, and in Japes opinion, Bombay represented the perfect fit to manage such a difficult hotel. They both loved to drink gin and fine wine, but Bombay stood in a league all his own when it came to total consumption. Working well together as a team, despite having different backgrounds and personalities proved vital when presented with one of the biggest challenges any business could face, and they dealt with it on their own. All-in would have provided great support during the upcoming months, but, as expected, Pan-face asked questions and provided no answers. He proved to be the king of boondoggles and would weekly write ridiculous stories related to the hotel industry. Apparently, the new wave in executive thinking involved not actually speaking with servers, but to write quasi-relevant hyperbole.

Summoned to the boardroom one day for a meeting with the Secret Service, an American Express representative, a MasterCard representative, and a Visa representative, thrust them into the world of cyber crime. The hotel computer system had been compromised and thousands of individual credit card numbers were stolen. These credit cards were used all over the world and would cost the credit card companies tens of thousands of dollars in retribution to the actual cardholders. The Secret Service agent, who looked more like a cover girl than an agent, implied it unlikely the perpetrator would actually be caught. The cyber attack marked something new to the world and extremely hard to track. Receiving a fine in the amount of a quarter-million dollars to be held in escrow abruptly ended the brief gathering. He did not realize the company transferring the funds from the hotel to the bank would arbitrarily take the money. In essence, the hotel received no revenue from its credit card transactions for nearly two weeks. The hotel contracted one of the few firms in the country to come into the hotel and analyze the data breach, which in turn would then report directly to the Secret Service, the franchise, and to the credit card companies. The young four-eyed geek, who flew in from the Midland Region carried the key to unlock the mystery. A typical nerd analyst, knowing the ins and outs of all the computer systems, Japes worked him as best he could, establishing a quick relationship while attempting to decipher what happened. Although the youngster could not say officially what occurred, he soon recognized the malignant software cleverly attached through the Internet onto the hotel's computer. He recognized this program from another hotel and showed Japes how access was made from the parent companies reservation system. The Crossroads Hotel in and of itself did not allow the breach, but the franchise, which the Crossroads annually paid hundreds of thousands of dollars in fees' appeared culpable. Furthermore, these breaches happened at many other franchised hotels throughout the country. Despite not being culpable the hotel made many physical and technical changes at its own expense, to essentially protect itself from the franchise. This was probably not a good sign when a business had to protect itself from the entity that set the standards.

Of course, Scrooge and his lawyers constantly bugged Bombay as the hotel progressed through this process. Japes and the accountants decided not to pay the franchise fees until the amount equaled the quarter million dollars in lost revenue. They would let the lawyers fight it out as to who owned the liability for the breach, but in the end the franchise made the Crossroads Hotel whole again. The franchise, fined five million dollars and spending millions more on correcting the reservation system, kept it all under the radar. Funny thing, despite the fact that Japes and Bombay had nothing to do with the breach, the two received no thank you for handling the crisis. They were rewarded with increased workloads and responsibilities.

Since Japes and the other controllers were no longer involved with the development of the company their role was defined for them as policemen. Their job included telling ownership about anything and everything that happened at the hotels, especially if there might be exposure to the ownership. In this new role they would be given no additional authority, no additional income, and in fact the compensation would go down over the years. The arrogant Scrooge and his associates became bureaucratic geniuses and now they had Pan-face, the puppet, at their beckoning call. Japes found sanctuary many mornings sitting in the sales office with his friends Peril and Dish. Peril and Dish were sales managers who had been promoted within the property, and had been employed for more than a decade. Japes would have his morning coffee and discuss anything except work. It highlighted a small ritual that he previously engaged in when he managed the Oasis, and he truly needed the personal exchanges and the sharing of each server's life outside of work. He knew that Pan-face frowned upon such behavior, but truly didn't give a server's poop, as he also knew nothing would be done to stop him.

At this time his old friend Capes searching for a new job, managed to hook up with Bombay and knock out a deal. Reuniting with his old pal and introducing a normal server to the mix who realized the importance of perspective in a server's life, felt like a breath of fresh air. The most important activities that occurred on a day-to-day basis for all servers had nothing to do with putting money in a corporation's pocket.

Capes introduced a little bit of fun to the hotel servers, as everyone realized with the departure of All-in that they were truly on an island all alone. All-in exemplified a go-getter who would hunt down any lead for development and would actively manage the hotel division. With the new restrictions put in place, the poker games and the casino outings came to a sudden halt. There was no fun in the workplace and the message resonated loud and clear that morale carried no weight with ownership. Be that as it may, Capes came up with a fantastic idea of having a spring fishing derby to be held in the pond at the Crossroads. The teams were set up between all of the departments the grand prize trophy going to the department, which caught the greatest number of fish in one hour. Even Japes, who at this time needed a walker to get around, participated in the event. This tiny pond, filled with sunfish and a large number of small perch was rumored to be the home of some large bass, but nobody had ever caught one. Well, nearing the end of the competition, the sales department and housekeeping department were tied as they each had landed sixteen fish. Bombay, using Japes special plastic worms, made the catch of the day by landing a two and a half pound bass. It looked like Moby Dick compared to the other fish that had been caught that day. With less than a minute to go Peril screaming at the top of her lungs landed a catfish, which catapulted the sales department to victory in the first annual Crossroads Fishing Derby. Despite all the obvious obstacles and the change in leadership the true hotel servers managed to bring a smile to everyone's face. Of course Japes and Bombay thought the trophy should go to the largest fish, but that would have to be taken under advisement by the fishing committee.

It eroded into an uphill battle for poor Bombay as he truly stood as a server on his own. The Crossroads Hotel was not a financial windfall for the owners as the economy eroded and this tertiary market delivered only a shadow of what it had produced in its day. Bombay would tell Japes "We are just the diapers of the operation" and that is how they treat us. Even with a great attitude, it was difficult for the hotel executives to discuss with ownership anything, which did not relate to a return on investment. Japes forged the best relationship he could with a boss who lived three thousand miles away, and who rarely visited the property. How do you quantify the attitude and feelings of hundreds of servers who barely scrape enough money together to pay their bills to bean counters who only relate to numbers? Even Shekelhound who personified a bean counter himself would visit with and get to know the operational servers. The hotel, forced to cut back on any event that would cost money and not give a direct return, endured. The reductions included limiting the employee luncheons to once per quarter and the annual holiday party expenditure to less than one thousand dollars. The owners would also put on a wage freeze for nearly two years while escalating the server's expense for health care and other basic needs. Scrooge used to make an annual visit, but would never be seen on property again as he pushed his agenda of inequality and disrespect. In fact, the entire reporting structure became so laissez-faire that the hotel servers felt like everything lay on their shoulders. Japes knew it was a sad day when he received more compliments and satisfaction in dealing with the bank that held the note on the hotel than he did from the owners. The bankers, in fact, informed Japes that Scrooge, during the last financial meeting, told them they could repossess the hotel if they did not like the terms of the loan.

The wonderful hotel career that Japes jumped into nearly forty years ago had for the first time in his life become a job. He thought to himself, Scrooge and his cronies were not acting with any moral compass they were malicious. The rat that Japes dreamed about years ago at Grub-land said that all mankind would be saved because they would devour the true enemy. Japes, after all these years, came to the conclusion that all the germs and insects would not be mankind's demise, but the Scrooge's of the world that acted with these beliefs would end them all. His career was coming to an end simply because of his physical challenges. He thought, however, that he would finish out this run before going down a new path. After all, he and his coworkers were getting a paycheck and certainly the Crossroads would make a comeback to profitability.

Before the Fourth of July holiday, Bombay requested all staff members come to an early meeting. Everyone assumed the topics would involve the normal hotel affairs in preparation for a long and busy weekend. Pan-head, who never came to the staff meeting, attended along with the corporate HR representative. Pan-head announced to the entire staff that the hotel had been sold and that the new ownership would be taking over in six days. He knew nothing about the new ownership, but insisted that everyone would have a job. All the servers, including some who worked at the Crossroads for more than two decades, exploded with questions. The representative of the new ownership, a twenty two-year-old wearing a Bluetooth headset, in five minutes, managed to insult the accomplishments of the entire staff and shed no light on his company. Furthermore, the regional office, which had been there for over twenty-five years, was to be closed, and these controllers would be terminated. Deceit surrounded the transaction, and highlighted exactly what Japes father taught him when he was a child. For years the company had been preaching they wanted to grow and expand, but in all those years they managed to purchase only one new hotel. What they actually did was sell an asset, and discard the servers like so many pieces of trash. Even Bowser, the lawyer, knew about the sale but could not provide Japes and the gang a heads up.

Immediately after the meeting Japes was summoned to Pan-head's office for a conference call with the powers to be. They informed Japes of a few items that he needed to complete for the closing, and that the new owners wished for him to stay. Japes, familiar with the new owners, informed them that they sold the hotel to the worst quasi-management company in the land. The new owners held no infrastructure and earned a terrible reputation for running hotels into the ground. Offering the insurance policy or any competitive benefits which All-in provided, never would occur. What could anyone do in six days? He informed the arrogant group that effective immediately he would be retiring from the workforce. Summarily dismissed from the meeting, he soon thereafter packed up his bags and said his goodbyes. Not the way he visioned leaving his beloved career, but the road he took presented the only path left for him and his family.

THE GOOD LIFE

Don't feel bad for Japes as he rocks in his chair watching Sammy shoot hoops, while the cardinals and the squirrels' race around the towering pine trees across from his front porch. It has been a few years since retiring, and although he is far from naive he still shakes his head when reflecting on the vicious nature of the greed shown by those in the world outside of the hotel. Inherently, the essence of a hotel culture is in itself one of safety and comfort. Servers are a breed all their own with skills in many disciplines, all of which is aimed at bringing a smile and a sense of belonging to everyone not just a select few. Nurturing an extremely challenging skill and an equally satisfying career motivates the server. They do not gain the recognition that many other professions enjoy, but when one is presented with the "real thing" they will never forget the experience. In fact, most will not see it coming and will not know what transpired to make them feel so special.

What are the rewards for such a career? Well, whether you are a hunched over slow moving old server like Japes, or a young, vibrant, wide eyed go getter just starting on a journey there are many rewards, but the greatest is happiness. Hardly a day goes by when Japes and his wife don't laugh about one of the literally hundreds of "hotel stories" they shared. Ironically, back in the day, when his old buddy Sot actually did something truly remarkable, although Jules still says it was his wife's doing; ever since he introduced Japes to this five foot nine inch stunningly beautiful brunette in her white blouse, jeans, and white sneakers Japes has been happy. Whether it be one hundred true servers drinking every ounce of available alcohol and dancing till sunrise at their wedding, or the endless number of social gatherings with fellow servers for decades to come, life has been good. It is funny how one gets rewarded as a server.

Japes and Jules spent their early years boating in the ocean every summer. He bought a twenty-one foot cabin cruiser, which he docked in the slip right next to his friend. They were introduced to this fantastic world by another server, Mac, the engineer from the Harsh days. Cruising the bays outside of Cod City and fishing the shoals near the lighthouse embodied serenity and will forever be cherished.

They bought a wee house out in the burbs and raised two of the most beautiful children anyone could want. As he received in his youth, Japes gave his family the introduction to Conifer every summer and every Christmas. The boy, Peter, took to fishing as if it was in his genes. Winning the local fishing derby at the age of 5 with an 18-inch largemouth bass hooked him for life, and it took all he had to land the behemoth. The girl, Megan, gravitated to the sheer beauty of the area. She is a gifted painter and photographer with a great eye for the moment.

They all still spend time at Conifer as they fish from the dock or go for swims in the lake. Japes wheels around the compound on his scooter visiting with the Conifer community. Some have been there for generations and some only a few years. They always visit with UJ, his uncle, who has a summer getaway on the compound. The King of Grub enjoys a spectacular view of the entire mountain range highlighted in the foreground by a magnificent stainless steel tree. They do not indulge like they did in their youth, but there is always plenty of liquor and endless laughter. It is in every way one of the most beautiful spots in the world.

The rewards continue as visits from servers have been steady over the years, and Japes loves the company. Throwback and Chief visit a couple of times each month for a glass of gin and the usual banter concerning sports and politics. Chief is contemplating moving south for warmer weather. Throwback has three wonderful kids and is a great father. He keeps Japes in the loop informing about the latest in the business world.

Capes made the trek a couple of times. He remains as balanced and industrious as when they worked together. His son is an executive on Wall Street, and his daughter is an analyst for a Fortune Five Hundred company. He too is a proud father. Recently moved to a spectacular ocean side condo right near where Japes and Jules kept their boat. Capes and his wife are true servers and a great example of success.

The ladies Dish, Peril and June visited last summer for a little scallop and shrimp ceviche with a mimosa on the porch. It reminded him of their coffee breaks' at the Crossroads Hotel. Peril had become a new grandmother, Dish changed her career, and June continued to wind hers' down. It felt like no time had passed and they instantly reconnected. Japes bragged that he could get on his scooter and go to the little league fields to watch OH's children play ball, or go to the school and watch his daughter play lacrosse. These are true rewards.

Every Christmas, Japes and Jules celebrate with Bobebbie and BoBark from the Carolinas. They visit her dad over the holidays and make time for Japes. It is hands down the hardest they laugh for a few hours every year, as they are great friends and true servers with an endless sense of adventure.

Classee and Mike made a trip to the porch, and Classee looked exactly the same as when she worked at the Oasis. She is a wonderful leader and is blessed to have Mike as a partner. Politics always comes up with Classee and she likes Hillary. Japes is not sure she will further the black movement as much as Bernie, only time will tell. Classee reminds Japes of the servers who he worked with in

Grubland, sincere and thoughtful. Always curious, she sought Japes opinion of Bill Cosby, as she had partied many times in her youth at his home. Knowing a young girl from the City of Mountains who Cos dated some forty years ago gave him reason to think Bill's behavior a little suspect. One of Japes greatest cultural rewards has been his friendship with Classee and an introduction to the black community.

The Hotel world provided Japes all of these rewards and too many visits to mention. It instilled in him the drive to keep pursuing the discipline he honed for so many years. He stands on his soapbox when anyone will listen, as he believes the hotel culture is a story of fun and happiness. He envisions this gentry translating to the outside world as he slowly pushes forward.

All-in asked Japes if he had any regrets. Did he regret the Harsh Hotel days and the terrible working philosophy? Japes thought for a few minutes, and came to the conclusion that he did not regret those days, nor did he regret any of the other stops along the way. There was, however, the one girl who looked like Marilyn Monroe, whom he shared a day of skiing with some four decades ago. No romance; what the hell was he thinking!

Glossary

Bull	One who takes control, dominant personality
Racer	A fast paced gogetter, organized, energetic
Kiva	A 'suck up', one who ingratiates to power
Flathead	A numbers cruncher, conforming, reactive
Mentsch	A decent and responsible person
Influencer	One with the gift of persuasion
Conifer	A Maine resort
Mountain City	Denver
Badlands	Texas
Flatlands	Florida
Northland	Canada
Picklehead	A knucklehead with a PHD
Grubland	A university in the heart of Boston